DreamWorks

PENGUINS OF MADAGASCAR

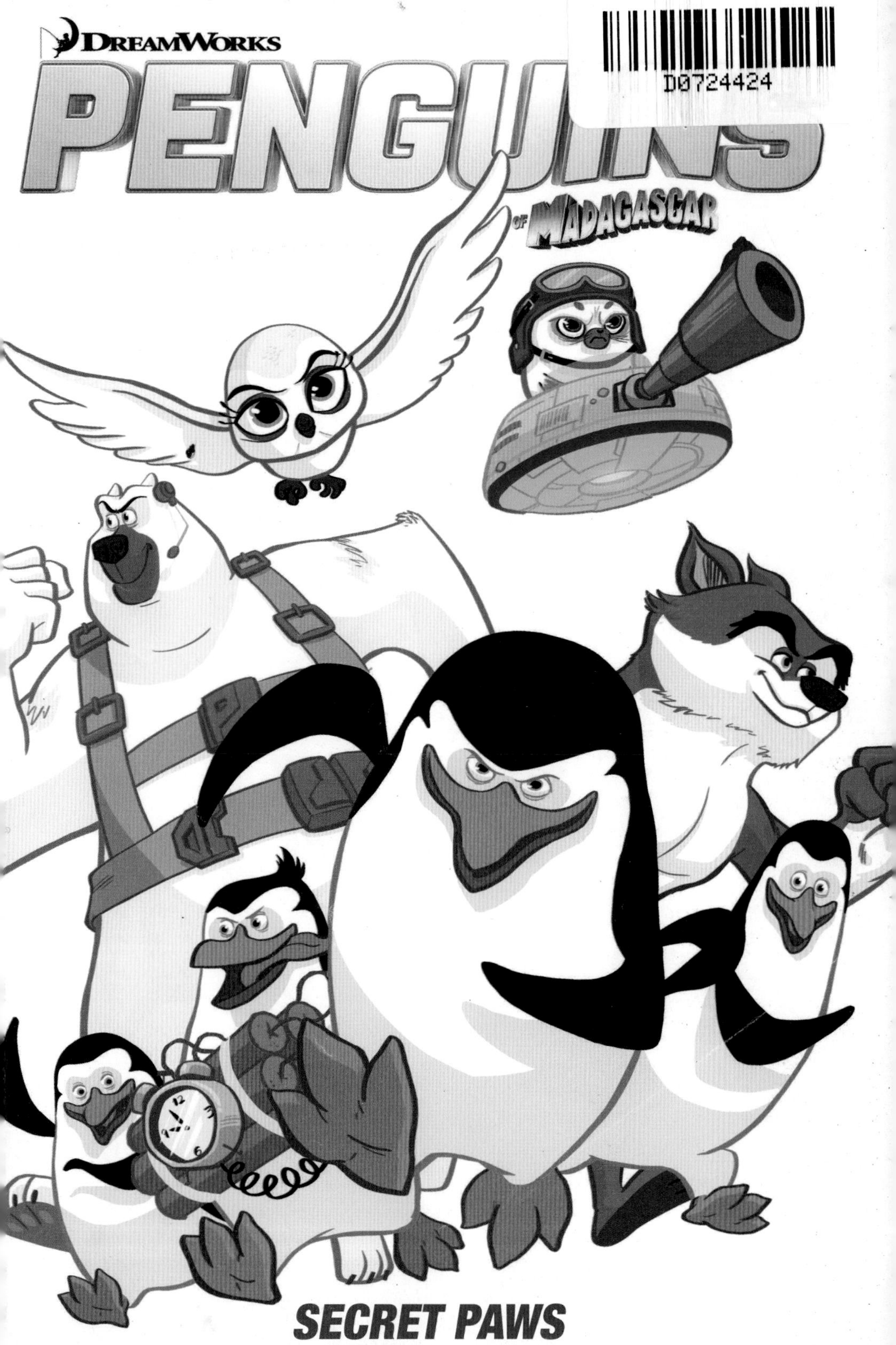

SECRET PAWS

THIS BOOK IS BROUGHT TO YOU BY...

Senior Editor Martin Eden
Production Manager Obi Onuora
Production Assistant Peter James
Production Supervisors
Jackie Flook, Maria Pearson
Studio Manager Emma Smith
Circulation Manager Steve Tothill
Direct Sales & Marketing Manager
Ricky Claydon
Publishing Manager Darryl Tothill
Publishing Director Chris Teather
Operations Director Leigh Baulch
Executive Director Vivian Cheung
Publisher Nick Landau

Penguins of Madagascar, Vol 4: Secret Paws
ISBN: 9781782762546

Penguins of Madagascar © 2016 DreamWorks Animation
LLC. All Rights Reserved. No part of this publication may
be reproduced, stored in a retrieval system, or transmitted,
in any form or by any means, without the prior written
permission of the publisher. Names, characters, places and
incidents featured in this publication are either the product
of the author's imagination or used fictitiously. Any
resemblance to actual persons, living or dead (except for
satirical purposes), is entirely coincidental.

10 9 8 7 6 5 4 3 2 1
First printed in Lithuania in August 2016.
A CIP catalogue record for this title is
available from the British Library.
TCN: 0560

Special thanks to Corinne Combs, Barbara Layman,
Lawrence Hamashima, and Mariko Yamashin.

DreamWorks

PENGUINS
of MADAGASCAR

Inside

2 EPIC COMIC STRIPS

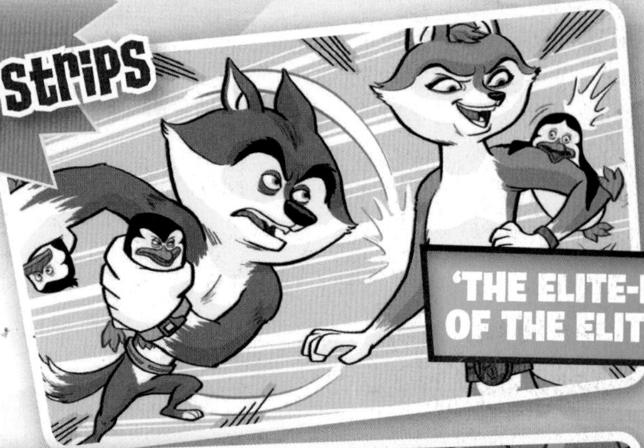

'THE ELITE-EST OF THE ELITE II'

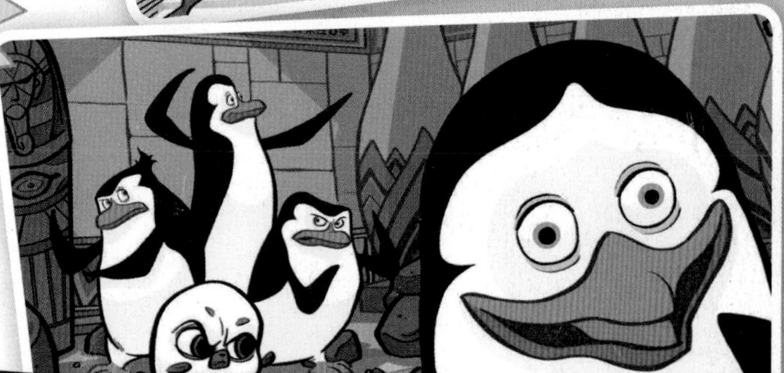

'ARCTIC FOXED'

Writer:
Cavan Scott
Art and colors:
Lucas Ferreyra
Letters:
Jim Campbell

Plus

THE NORTH WIND IN...

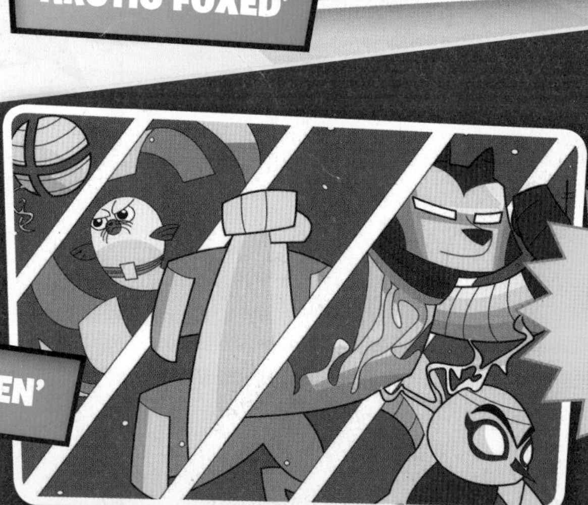

'BROKEN'

Writer:
David Baillie
Art and colors:
Grant Perkins
Letters:
Jim Campbell

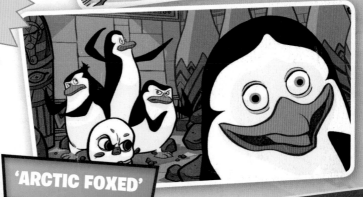

Meet the P
Madagascar!

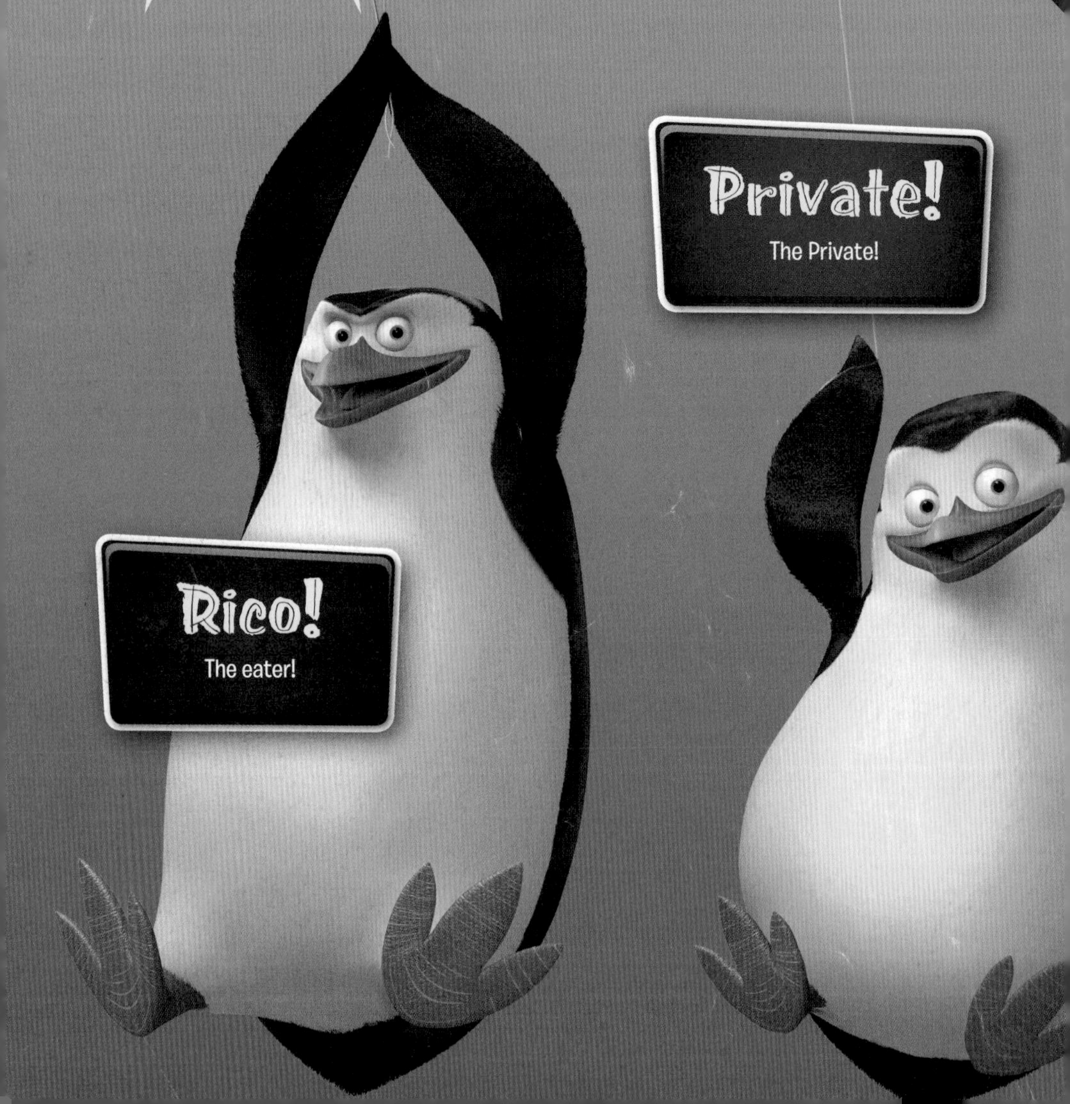
Private!
The Private!
Rico!
The eater!

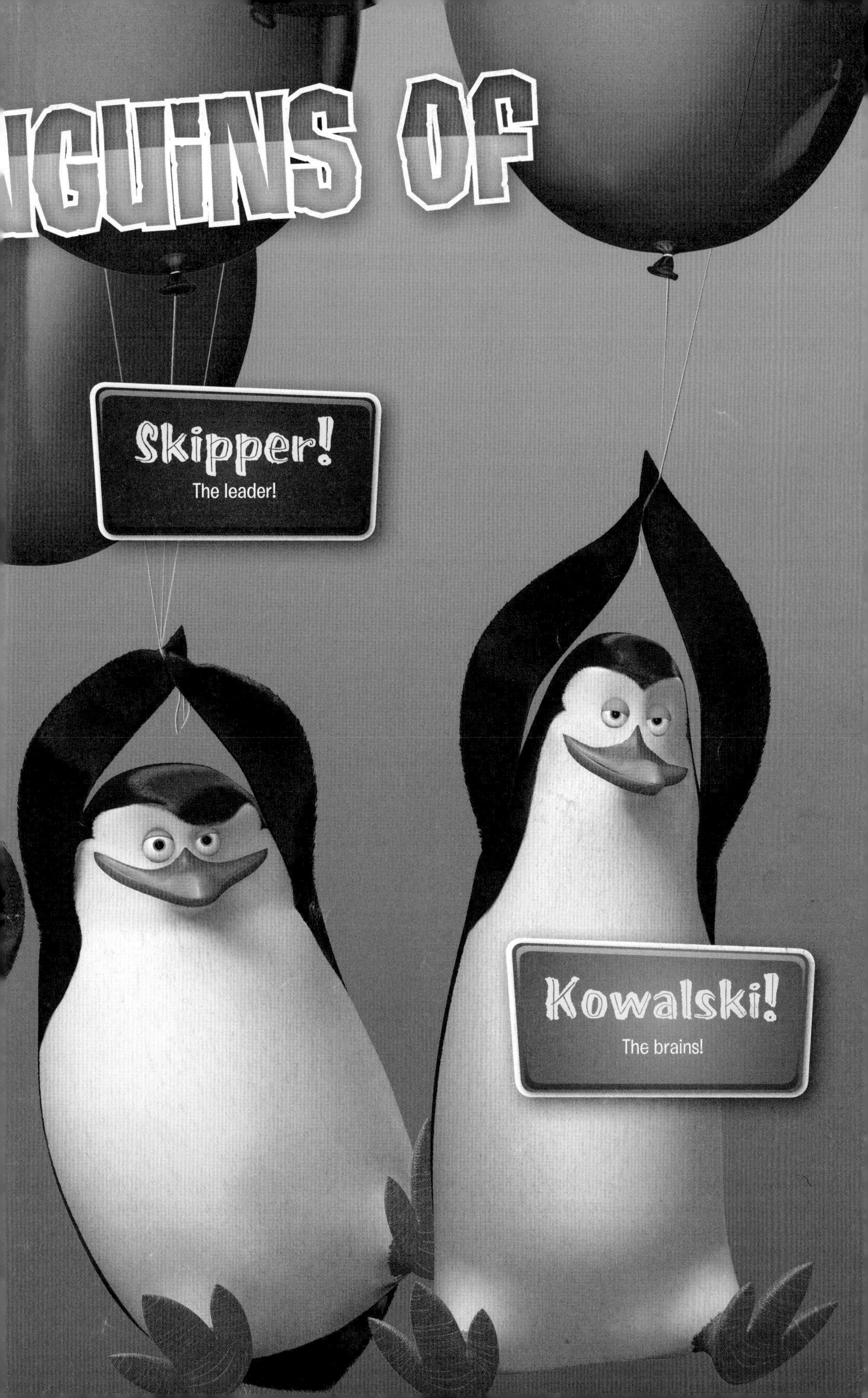
GUINS OF
Skipper!
The leader!
Kowalski!
The brains!

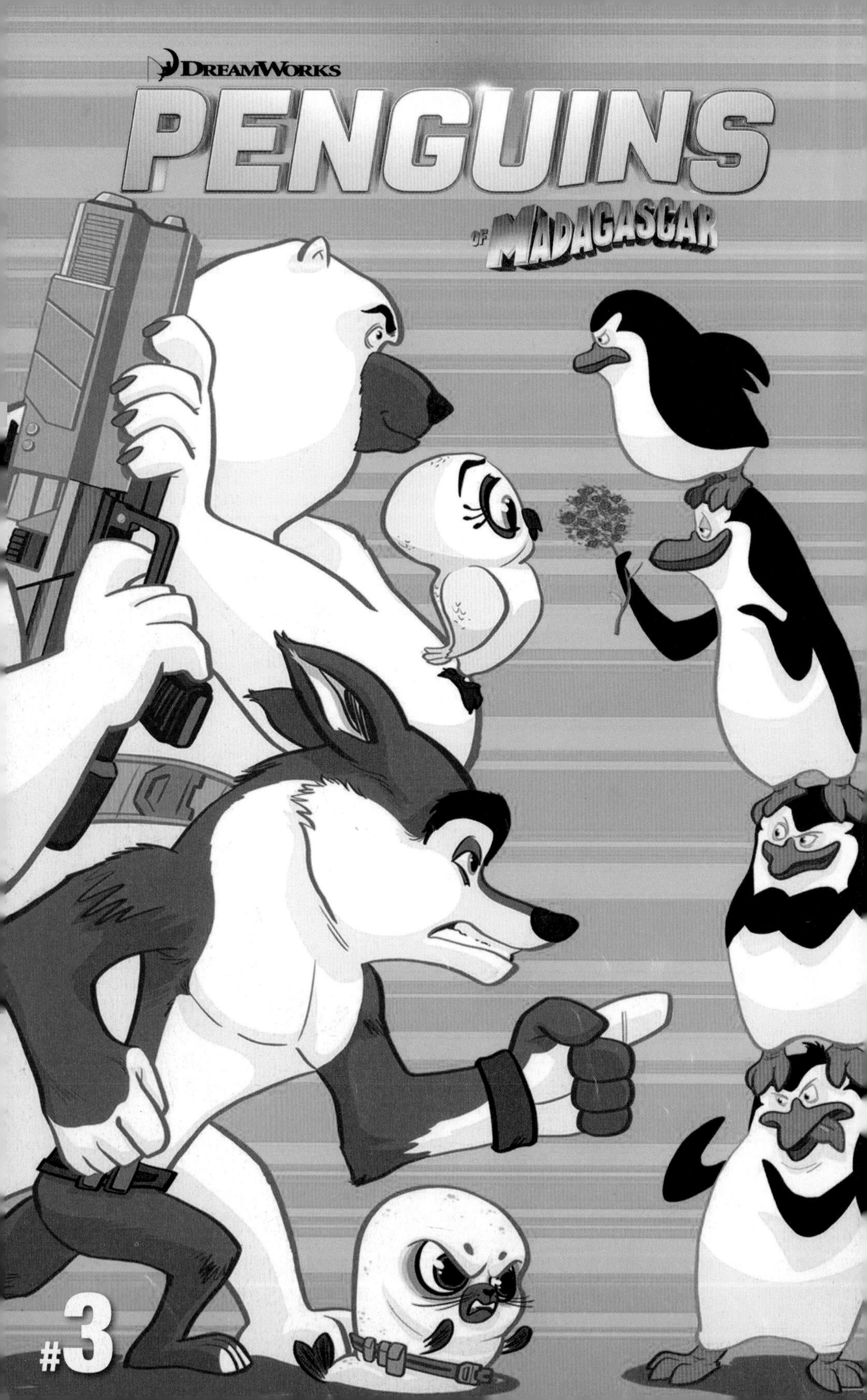

DREAMWORKS
PENGUINS
OF MADAGASCAR
#3

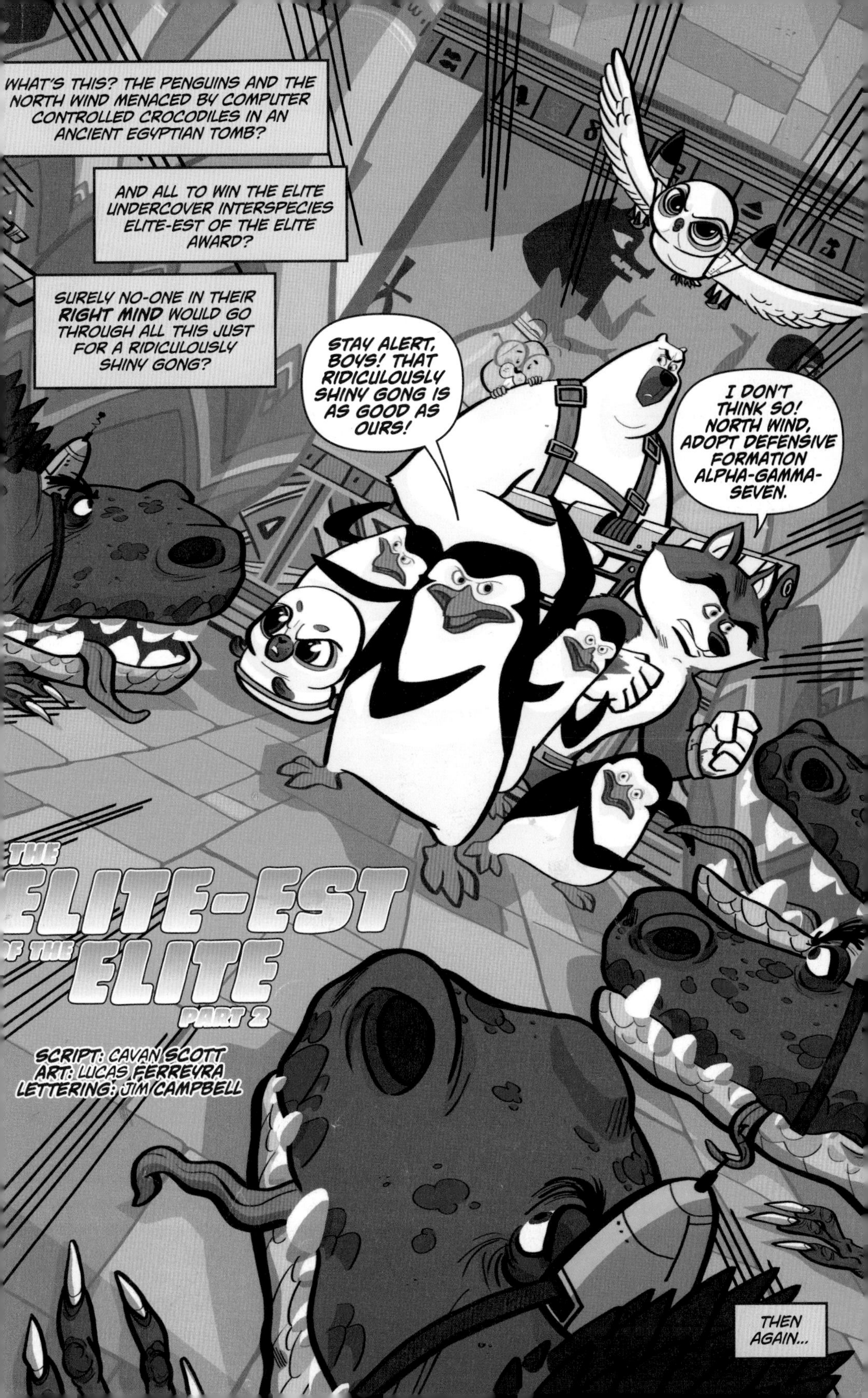

WHAT'S THIS? THE PENGUINS AND THE NORTH WIND MENACED BY COMPUTER CONTROLLED CROCODILES IN AN ANCIENT EGYPTIAN TOMB?
AND ALL TO WIN THE ELITE UNDERCOVER INTERSPECIES ELITE-EST OF THE ELITE AWARD?
SURELY NO-ONE IN THEIR **RIGHT MIND** WOULD GO THROUGH ALL THIS JUST FOR A RIDICULOUSLY SHINY GONG?
STAY ALERT, BOYS! THAT RIDICULOUSLY SHINY GONG IS AS GOOD AS OURS!
I DON'T THINK SO! NORTH WIND, ADOPT DEFENSIVE FORMATION ALPHA-GAMMA-SEVEN.
THE ELITE-EST OF THE ELITE PART 2
SCRIPT: CAVAN SCOTT
ART: LUCAS FERREYRA
LETTERING: JIM CAMPBELL
THEN AGAIN...

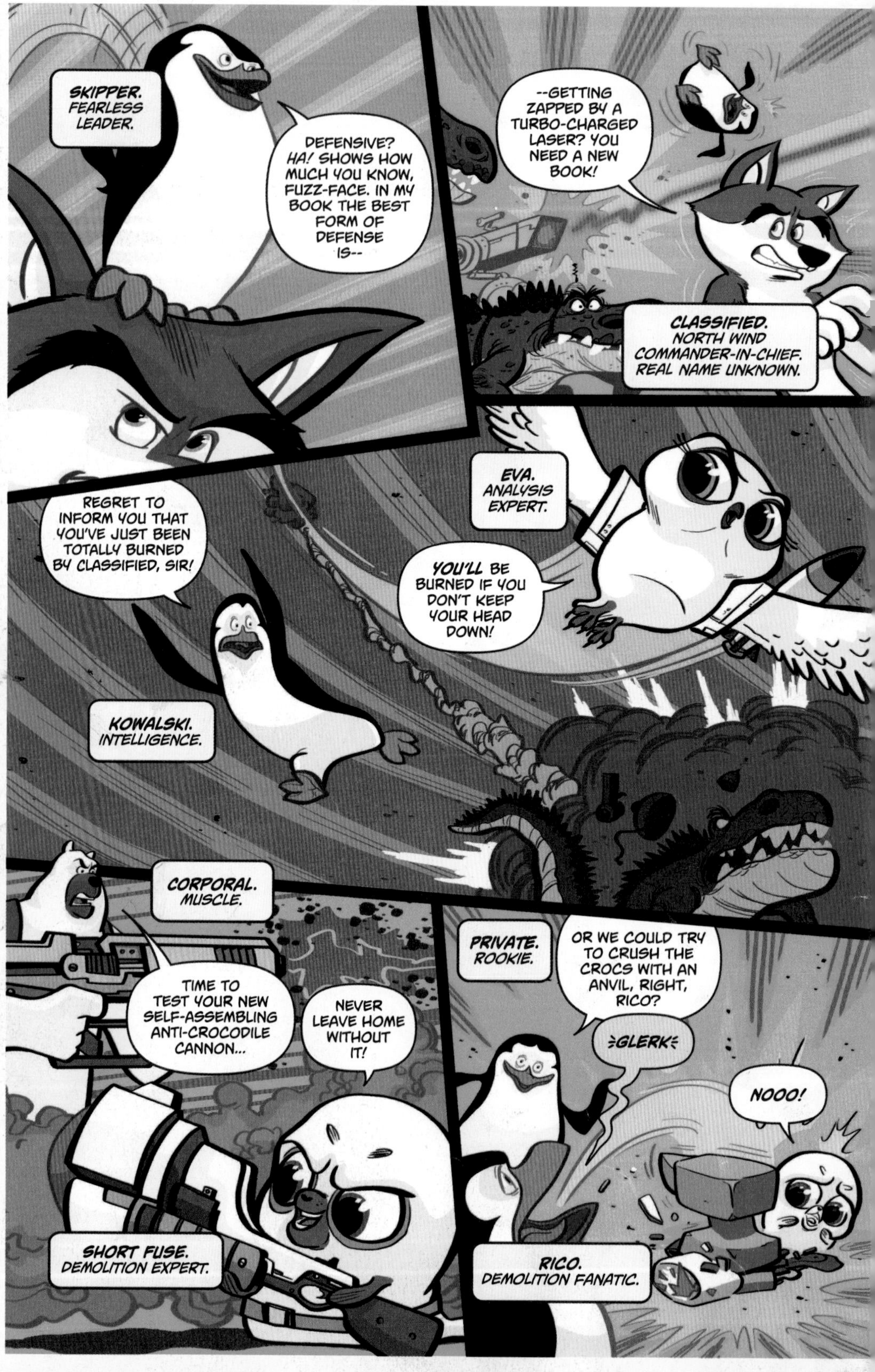
SKIPPER. FEARLESS LEADER.
DEFENSIVE? HA! SHOWS HOW MUCH YOU KNOW, FUZZ-FACE. IN MY BOOK THE BEST FORM OF DEFENSE IS--
--GETTING ZAPPED BY A TURBO-CHARGED LASER? YOU NEED A NEW BOOK!
CLASSIFIED. NORTH WIND COMMANDER-IN-CHIEF. REAL NAME UNKNOWN.
EVA. ANALYSIS EXPERT.
REGRET TO INFORM YOU THAT YOU'VE JUST BEEN TOTALLY BURNED BY CLASSIFIED, SIR!
YOU'LL BE BURNED IF YOU DON'T KEEP YOUR HEAD DOWN!
KOWALSKI. INTELLIGENCE.
CORPORAL. MUSCLE.
TIME TO TEST YOUR NEW SELF-ASSEMBLING ANTI-CROCODILE CANNON...
NEVER LEAVE HOME WITHOUT IT!
SHORT FUSE. DEMOLITION EXPERT.
PRIVATE. ROOKIE.
OR WE COULD TRY TO CRUSH THE CROCS WITH AN ANVIL, RIGHT, RICO?
GLERK
NOOO!
RICO. DEMOLITION FANATIC.

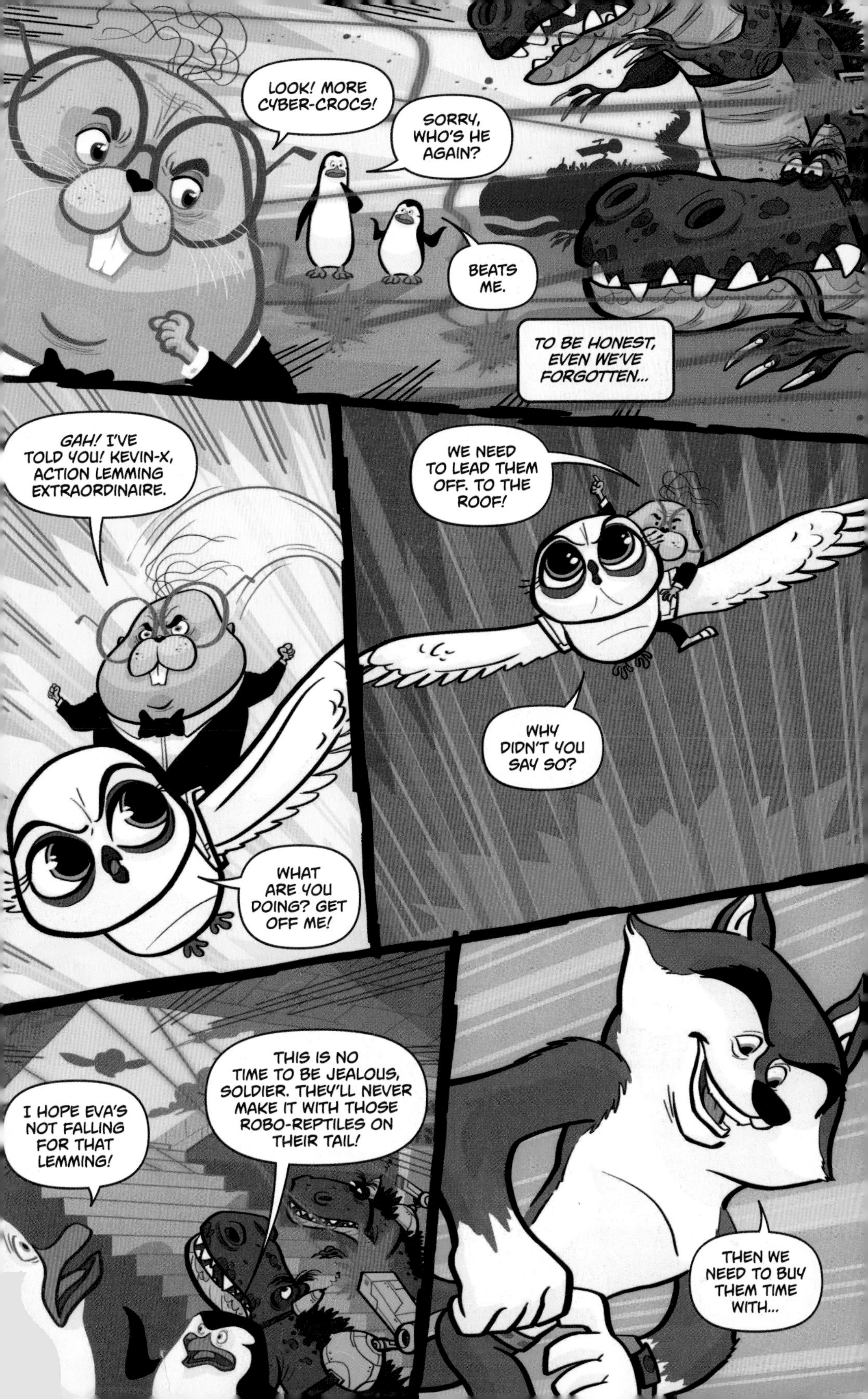
LOOK! MORE CYBER-CROCS!
SORRY, WHO'S HE AGAIN?
BEATS ME.
TO BE HONEST, EVEN WE'VE FORGOTTEN...
GAH! I'VE TOLD YOU! KEVIN-X, ACTION LEMMING EXTRAORDINAIRE.
WHAT ARE YOU DOING? GET OFF ME!
WE NEED TO LEAD THEM OFF. TO THE ROOF!
WHY DIDN'T YOU SAY SO?
I HOPE EVA'S NOT FALLING FOR THAT LEMMING!
THIS IS NO TIME TO BE JEALOUS, SOLDIER. THEY'LL NEVER MAKE IT WITH THOSE ROBO-REPTILES ON THEIR TAIL!
THEN WE NEED TO BUY THEM TIME WITH...

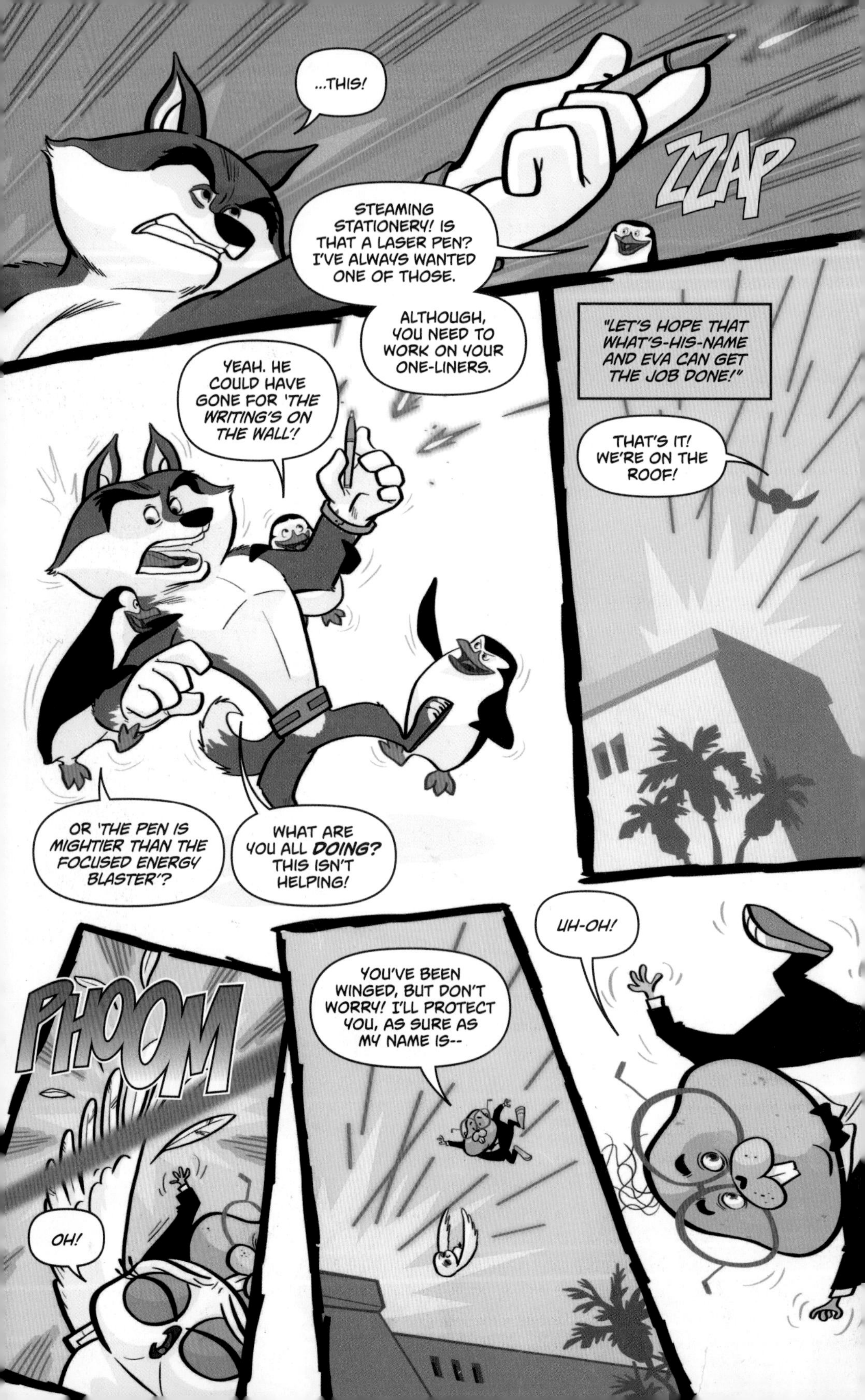
...THIS!
ZZAP
STEAMING STATIONERY! IS THAT A LASER PEN? I'VE ALWAYS WANTED ONE OF THOSE.
ALTHOUGH, YOU NEED TO WORK ON YOUR ONE-LINERS.
YEAH. HE COULD HAVE GONE FOR 'THE WRITING'S ON THE WALL'!
OR 'THE PEN IS MIGHTIER THAN THE FOCUSED ENERGY BLASTER'?
WHAT ARE YOU ALL DOING? THIS ISN'T HELPING!
"LET'S HOPE THAT WHAT'S-HIS-NAME AND EVA CAN GET THE JOB DONE!"
THAT'S IT! WE'RE ON THE ROOF!
PHOOM
OH!
YOU'VE BEEN WINGED, BUT DON'T WORRY! I'LL PROTECT YOU, AS SURE AS MY NAME IS--
UH-OH!

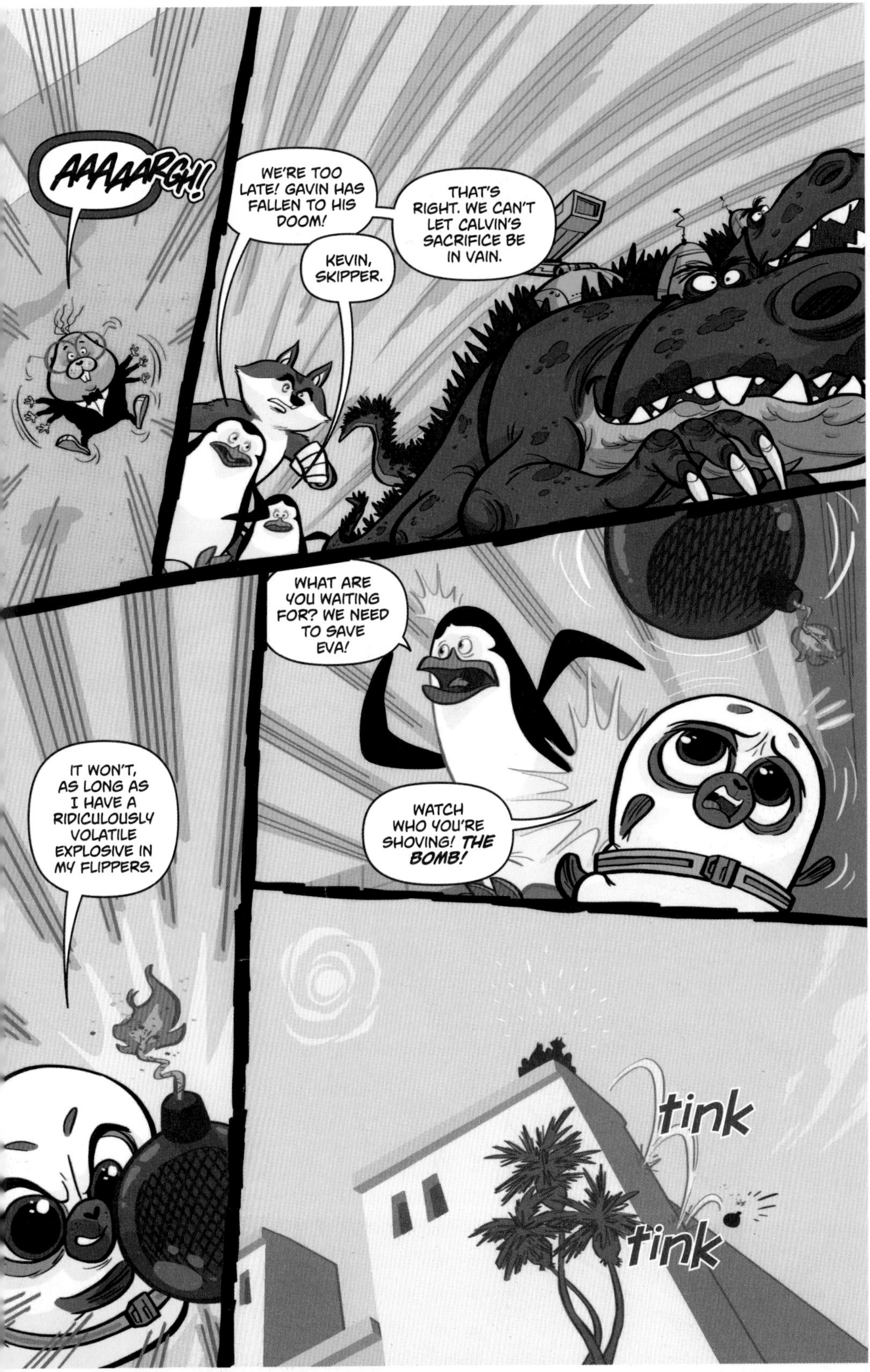
AAAAARGH!
WE'RE TOO LATE! GAVIN HAS FALLEN TO HIS DOOM!
KEVIN, SKIPPER.
THAT'S RIGHT. WE CAN'T LET CALVIN'S SACRIFICE BE IN VAIN.
WHAT ARE YOU WAITING FOR? WE NEED TO SAVE EVA!
WATCH WHO YOU'RE SHOVING! THE BOMB!
IT WON'T, AS LONG AS I HAVE A RIDICULOUSLY VOLATILE EXPLOSIVE IN MY FLIPPERS.
tink
tink

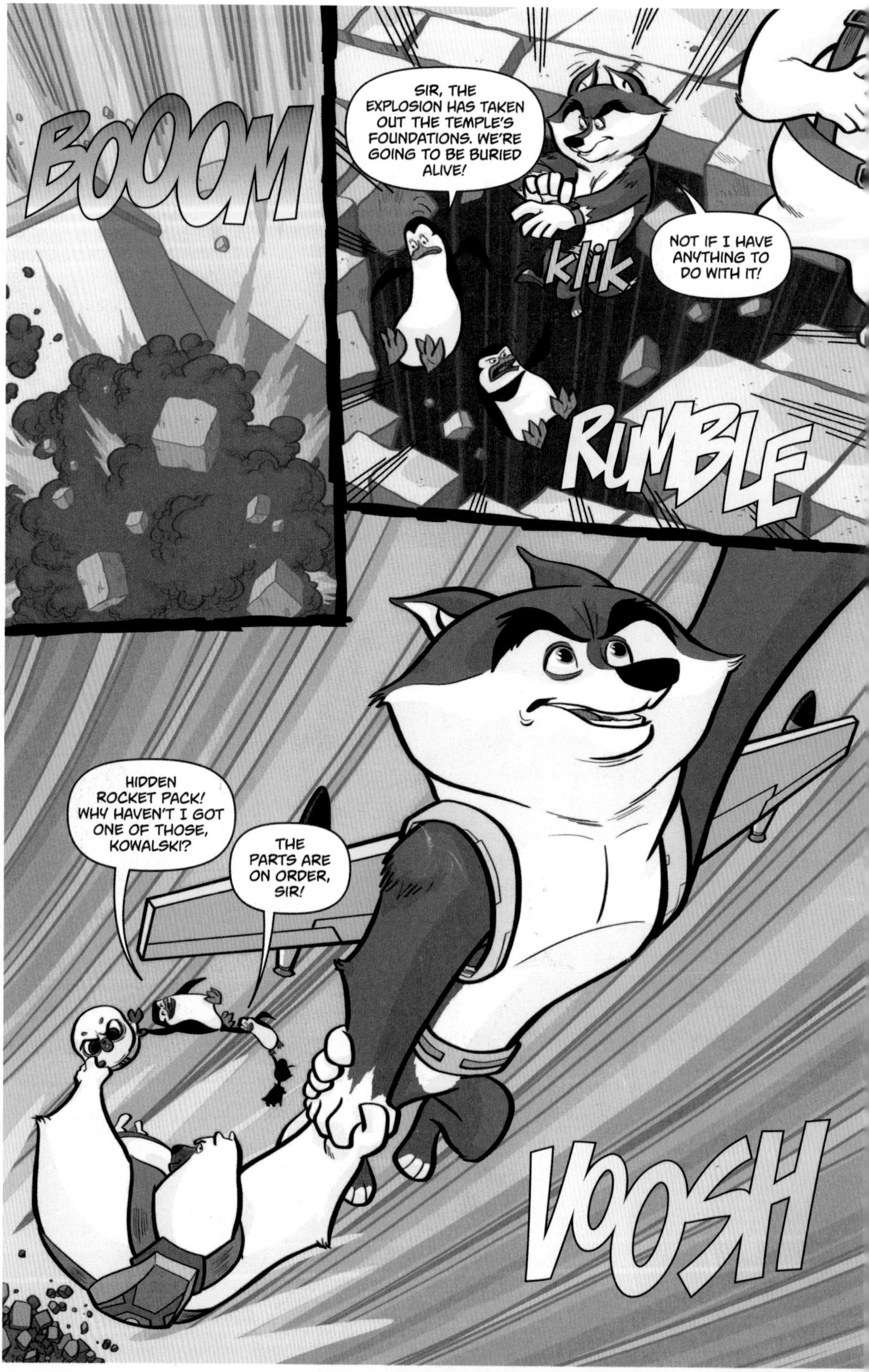
BOOOM
SIR, THE EXPLOSION HAS TAKEN OUT THE TEMPLE'S FOUNDATIONS. WE'RE GOING TO BE BURIED ALIVE!
KLIK
NOT IF I HAVE ANYTHING TO DO WITH IT!
RUMBLE
HIDDEN ROCKET PACK! WHY HAVEN'T I GOT ONE OF THOSE, KOWALSKI?
THE PARTS ARE ON ORDER, SIR!
VOOSH

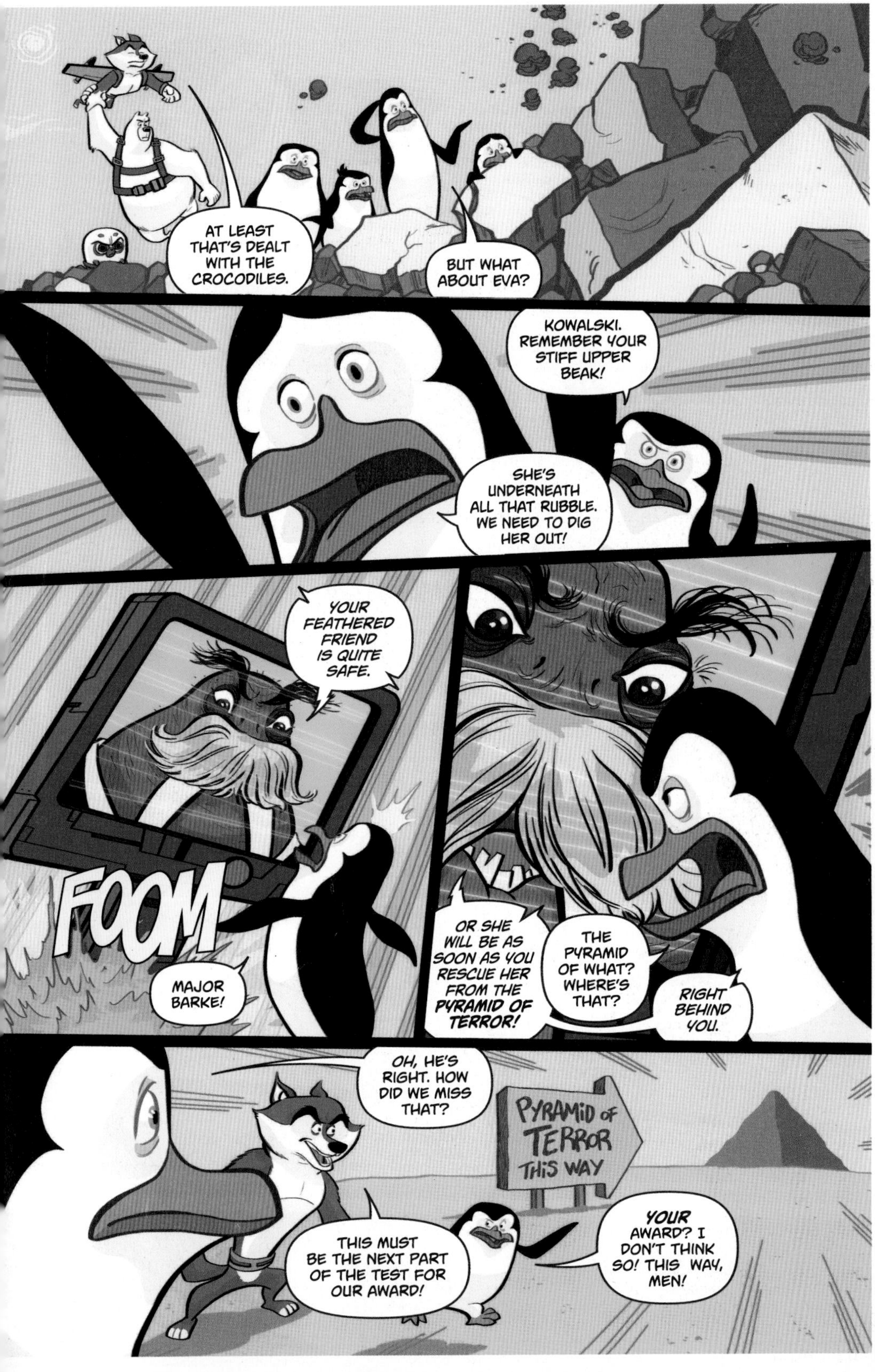
AT LEAST THAT'S DEALT WITH THE CROCODILES.
BUT WHAT ABOUT EVA?
KOWALSKI. REMEMBER YOUR STIFF UPPER BEAK!
SHE'S UNDERNEATH ALL THAT RUBBLE. WE NEED TO DIG HER OUT!
YOUR FEATHERED FRIEND IS QUITE SAFE.
FOOM
MAJOR BARKE!
OR SHE WILL BE AS SOON AS YOU RESCUE HER FROM THE PYRAMID OF TERROR!
THE PYRAMID OF WHAT? WHERE'S THAT?
RIGHT BEHIND YOU.
OH, HE'S RIGHT. HOW DID WE MISS THAT?
PYRAMID OF TERROR THIS WAY
THIS MUST BE THE NEXT PART OF THE TEST FOR OUR AWARD!
YOUR AWARD? I DON'T THINK SO! THIS WAY, MEN!

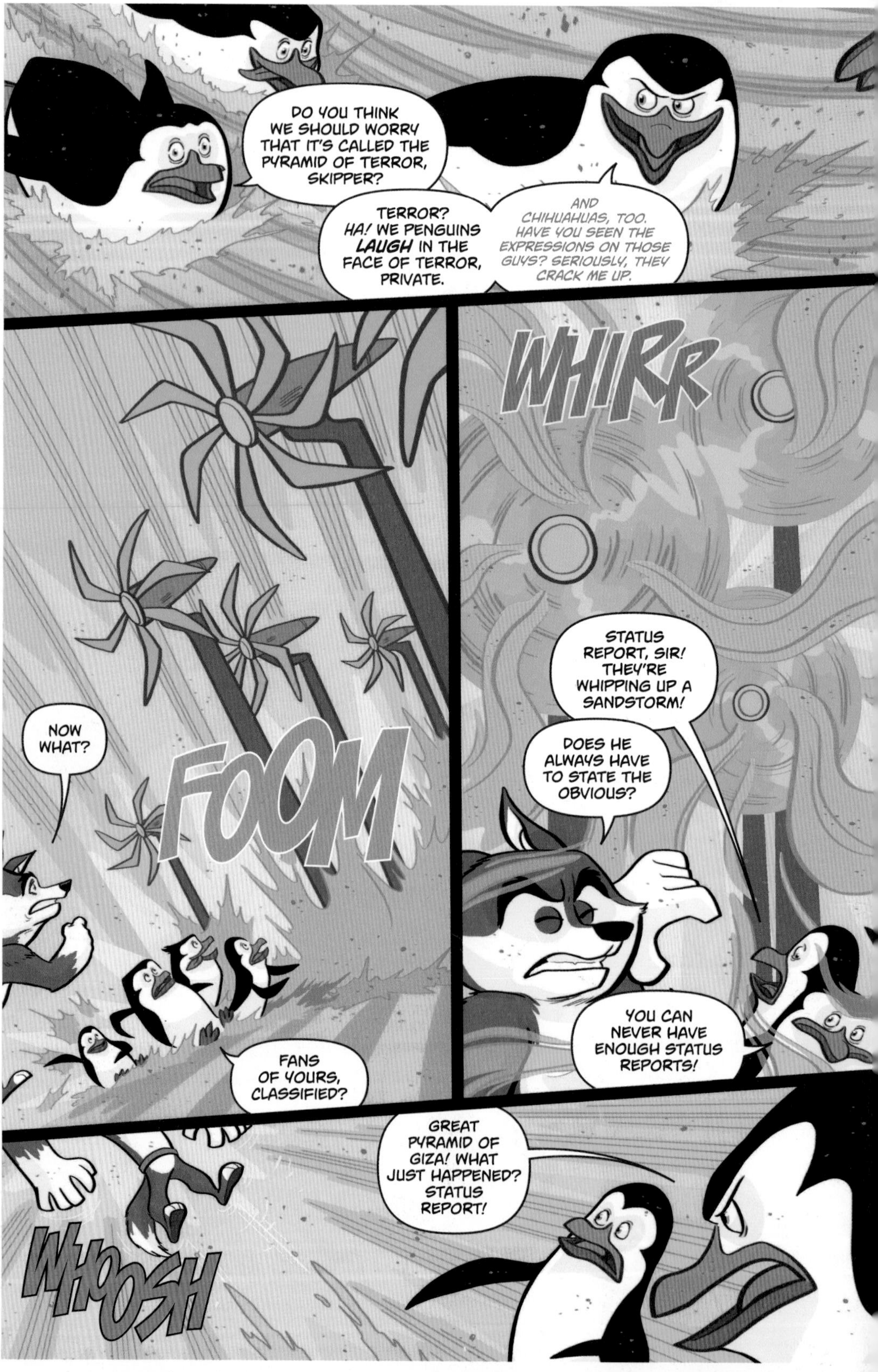
DO YOU THINK WE SHOULD WORRY THAT IT'S CALLED THE PYRAMID OF TERROR, SKIPPER?
TERROR? HA! WE PENGUINS **LAUGH** IN THE FACE OF TERROR, PRIVATE.
AND CHIHUAHUAS, TOO. HAVE YOU SEEN THE EXPRESSIONS ON THOSE GUYS? SERIOUSLY, THEY CRACK ME UP.
NOW WHAT?
FOOM
FANS OF YOURS, CLASSIFIED?
WHIRR
STATUS REPORT, SIR! THEY'RE WHIPPING UP A SANDSTORM!
DOES HE ALWAYS HAVE TO STATE THE OBVIOUS?
YOU CAN NEVER HAVE ENOUGH STATUS REPORTS!
WHOOSH
GREAT PYRAMID OF GIZA! WHAT JUST HAPPENED? STATUS REPORT!

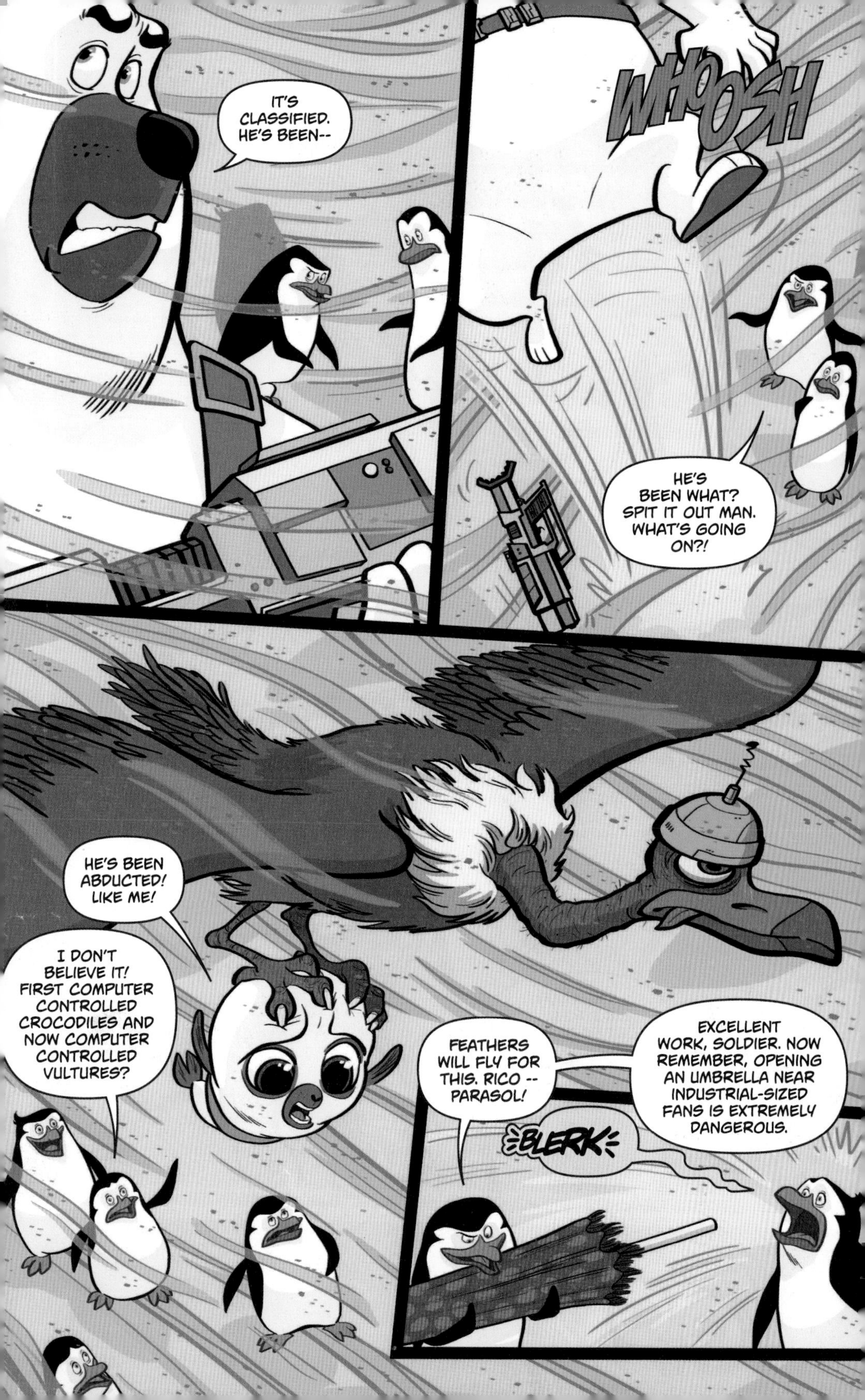
IT'S CLASSIFIED. HE'S BEEN--
WHOOSH
HE'S BEEN WHAT? SPIT IT OUT MAN. WHAT'S GOING ON?!
HE'S BEEN ABDUCTED! LIKE ME!
I DON'T BELIEVE IT! FIRST COMPUTER CONTROLLED CROCODILES AND NOW COMPUTER CONTROLLED VULTURES?
FEATHERS WILL FLY FOR THIS. RICO -- PARASOL!
BLERK
EXCELLENT WORK, SOLDIER. NOW REMEMBER, OPENING AN UMBRELLA NEAR INDUSTRIAL-SIZED FANS IS EXTREMELY DANGEROUS.

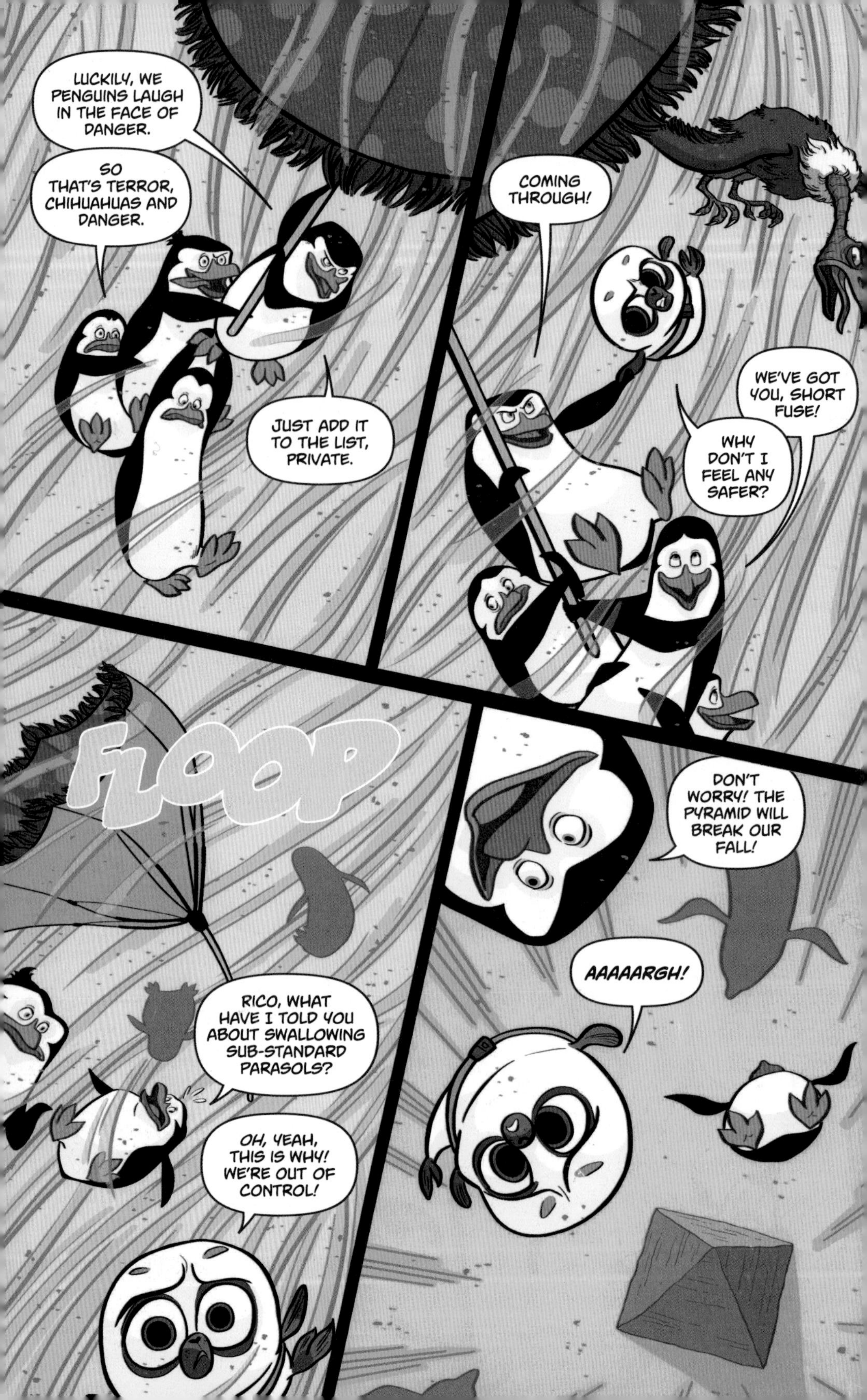
LUCKILY, WE PENGUINS LAUGH IN THE FACE OF DANGER.
SO THAT'S TERROR, CHIHUAHUAS AND DANGER.
JUST ADD IT TO THE LIST, PRIVATE.
COMING THROUGH!
WE'VE GOT YOU, SHORT FUSE!
WHY DON'T I FEEL ANY SAFER?
FLOOP
RICO, WHAT HAVE I TOLD YOU ABOUT SWALLOWING SUB-STANDARD PARASOLS?
OH, YEAH, THIS IS WHY! WE'RE OUT OF CONTROL!
DON'T WORRY! THE PYRAMID WILL BREAK OUR FALL!
AAAAARGH!

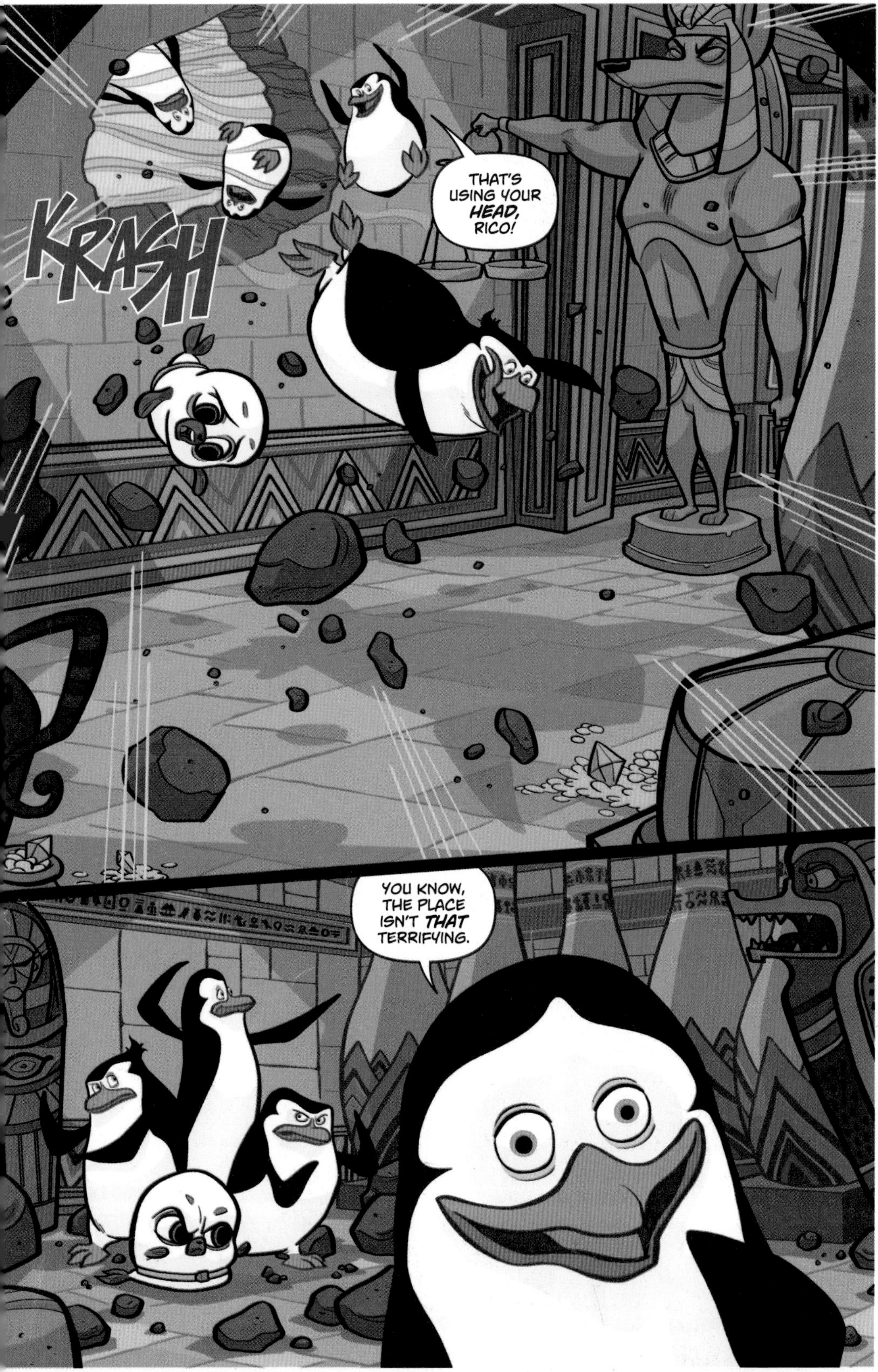
KRASH
THAT'S USING YOUR HEAD, RICO!
YOU KNOW, THE PLACE ISN'T THAT TERRIFYING.

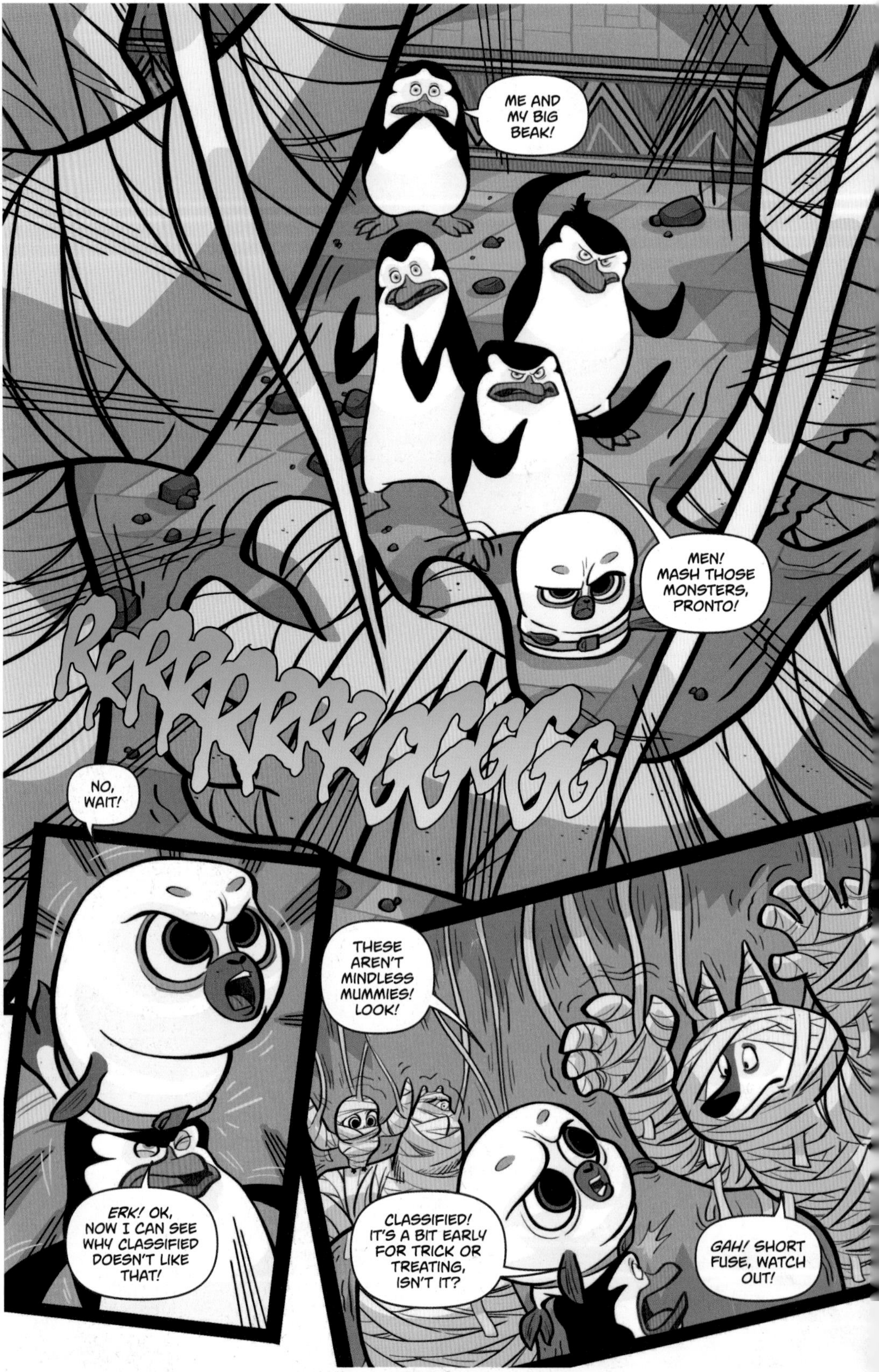
ME AND MY BIG BEAK!
MEN! MASH THOSE MONSTERS, PRONTO!
RRRRRRRRRRGGGGG
NO, WAIT!
ERK! OK, NOW I CAN SEE WHY CLASSIFIED DOESN'T LIKE THAT!
THESE AREN'T MINDLESS MUMMIES! LOOK!
CLASSIFIED! IT'S A BIT EARLY FOR TRICK OR TREATING, ISN'T IT?
GAH! SHORT FUSE, WATCH OUT!

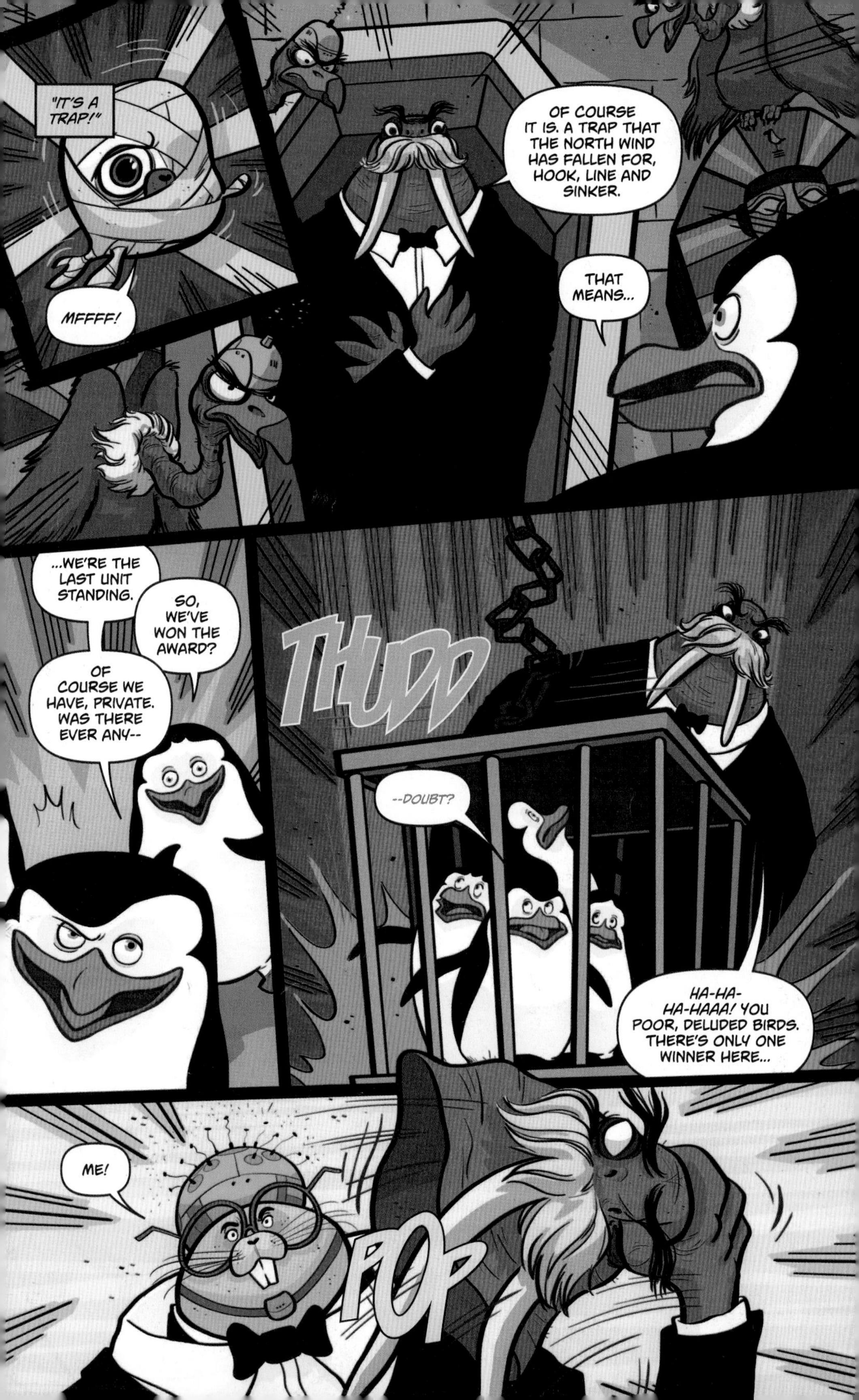
"IT'S A TRAP!"
MFFFF!
OF COURSE IT IS. A TRAP THAT THE NORTH WIND HAS FALLEN FOR, HOOK, LINE AND SINKER.
THAT MEANS...
...WE'RE THE LAST UNIT STANDING.
SO, WE'VE WON THE AWARD?
OF COURSE WE HAVE, PRIVATE. WAS THERE EVER ANY--
THUDD
--DOUBT?
HA-HA-HA-HAAA! YOU POOR, DELUDED BIRDS. THERE'S ONLY ONE WINNER HERE...
ME!
POP

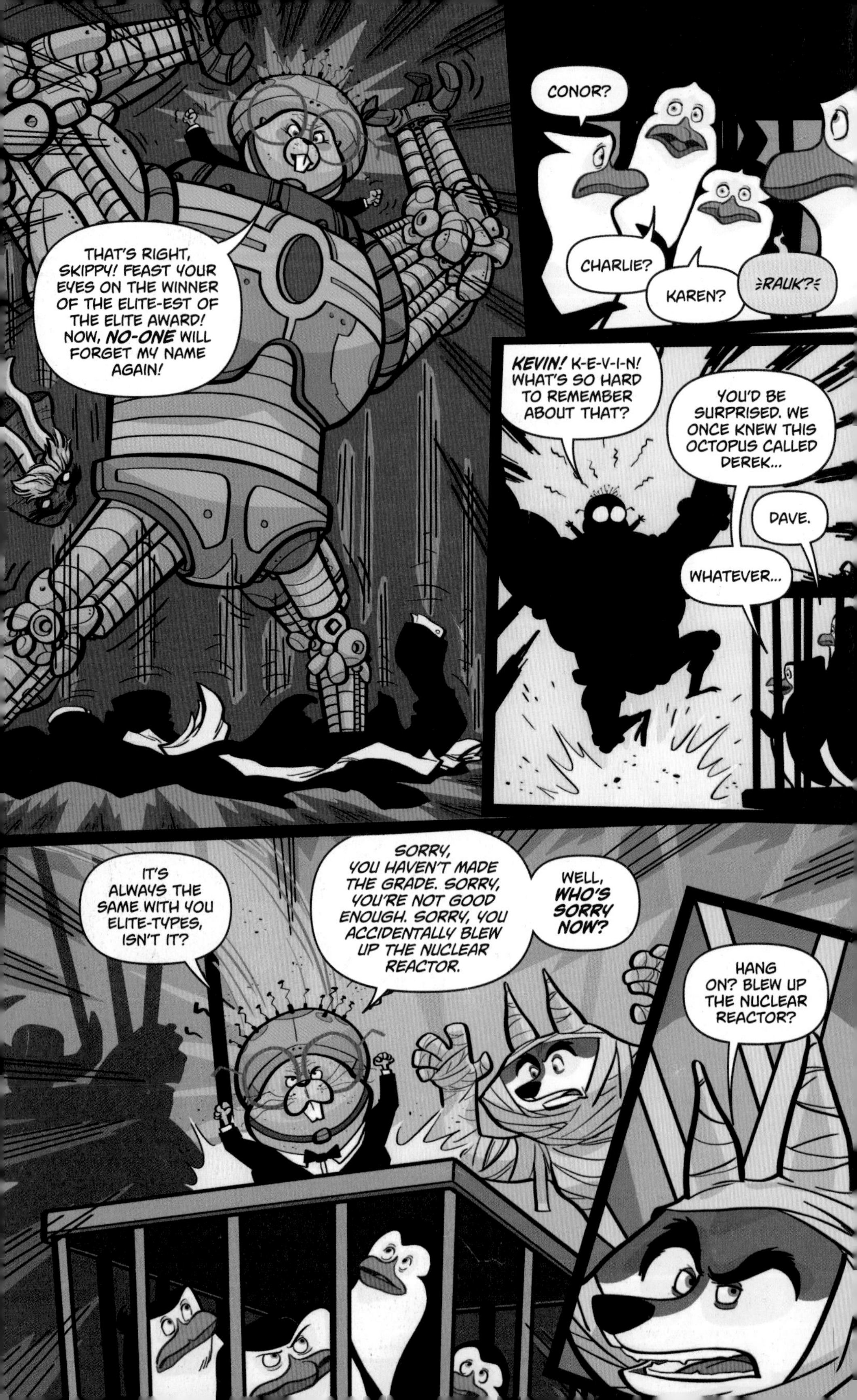
THAT'S RIGHT, SKIPPY! FEAST YOUR EYES ON THE WINNER OF THE ELITE-EST OF THE ELITE AWARD! NOW, NO-ONE WILL FORGET MY NAME AGAIN!
CONOR?
CHARLIE?
KAREN?
RAUK?
KEVIN! K-E-V-I-N! WHAT'S SO HARD TO REMEMBER ABOUT THAT?
YOU'D BE SURPRISED. WE ONCE KNEW THIS OCTOPUS CALLED DEREK...
DAVE.
WHATEVER...
IT'S ALWAYS THE SAME WITH YOU ELITE-TYPES, ISN'T IT?
SORRY, YOU HAVEN'T MADE THE GRADE. SORRY, YOU'RE NOT GOOD ENOUGH. SORRY, YOU ACCIDENTALLY BLEW UP THE NUCLEAR REACTOR.
WELL, WHO'S SORRY NOW?
HANG ON? BLEW UP THE NUCLEAR REACTOR?

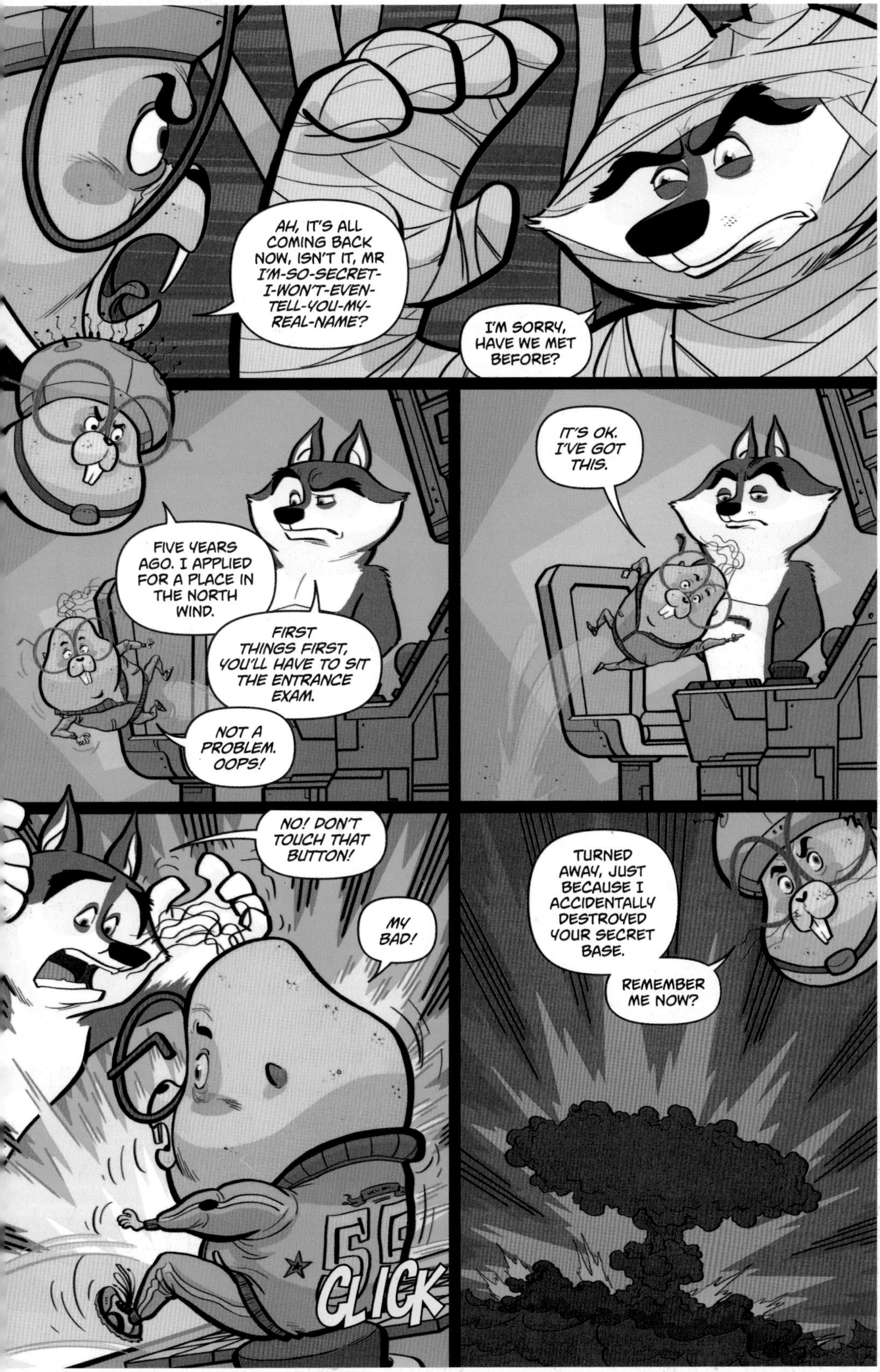
AH, IT'S ALL COMING BACK NOW, ISN'T IT, MR I'M-SO-SECRET-I-WON'T-EVEN-TELL-YOU-MY-REAL-NAME?
I'M SORRY, HAVE WE MET BEFORE?
FIVE YEARS AGO. I APPLIED FOR A PLACE IN THE NORTH WIND.
FIRST THINGS FIRST, YOU'LL HAVE TO SIT THE ENTRANCE EXAM.
NOT A PROBLEM. OOPS!
IT'S OK. I'VE GOT THIS.
NO! DON'T TOUCH THAT BUTTON!
MY BAD!
CLICK
TURNED AWAY, JUST BECAUSE I ACCIDENTALLY DESTROYED YOUR SECRET BASE.
REMEMBER ME NOW?

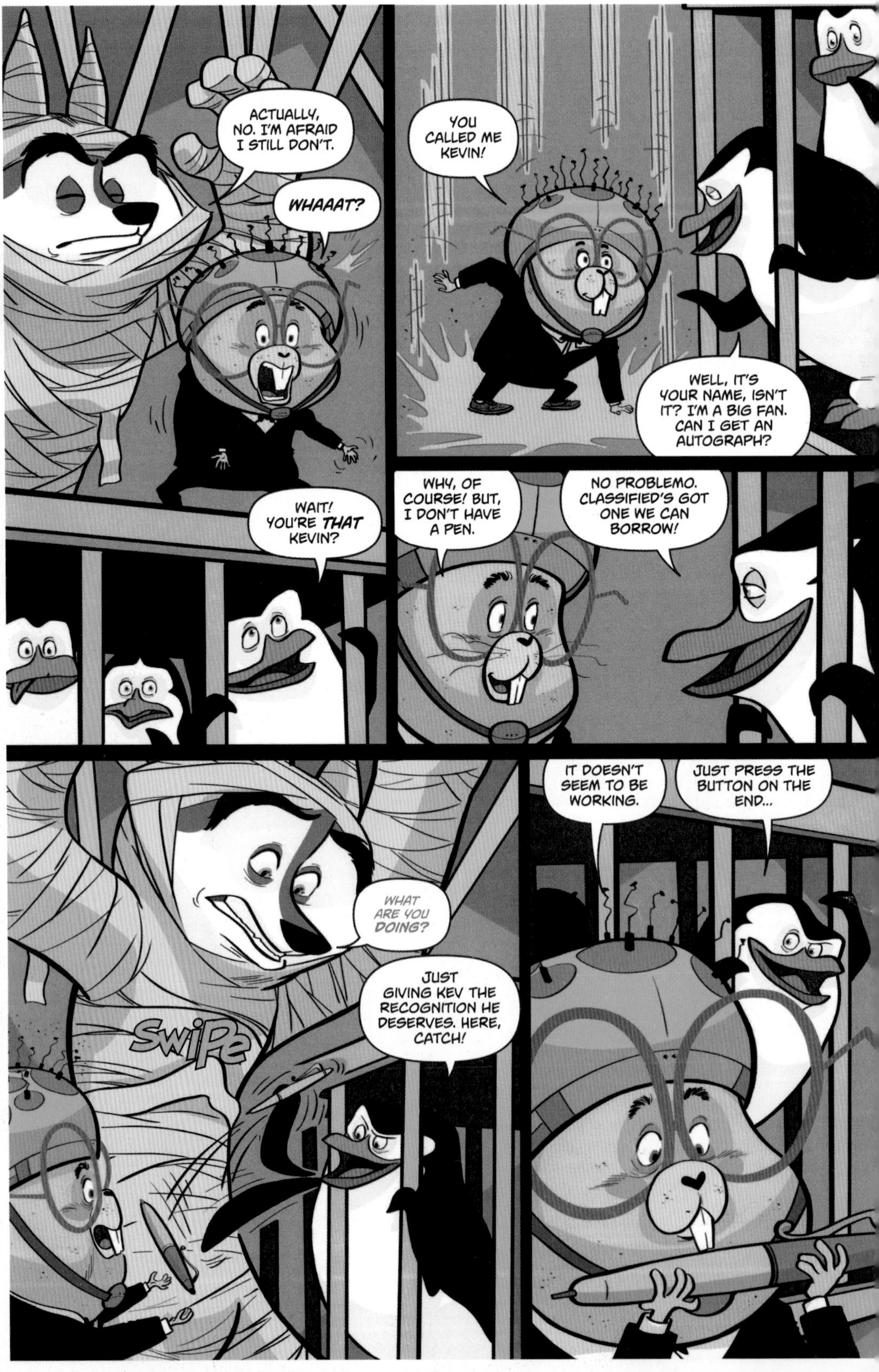
ACTUALLY, NO. I'M AFRAID I STILL DON'T.
WHAAAT?
YOU CALLED ME KEVIN!
WELL, IT'S YOUR NAME, ISN'T IT? I'M A BIG FAN. CAN I GET AN AUTOGRAPH?
WAIT! YOU'RE THAT KEVIN?
WHY, OF COURSE! BUT, I DON'T HAVE A PEN.
NO PROBLEMO. CLASSIFIED'S GOT ONE WE CAN BORROW!
WHAT ARE YOU DOING?
JUST GIVING KEV THE RECOGNITION HE DESERVES. HERE, CATCH!
SWIPE
IT DOESN'T SEEM TO BE WORKING.
JUST PRESS THE BUTTON ON THE END...

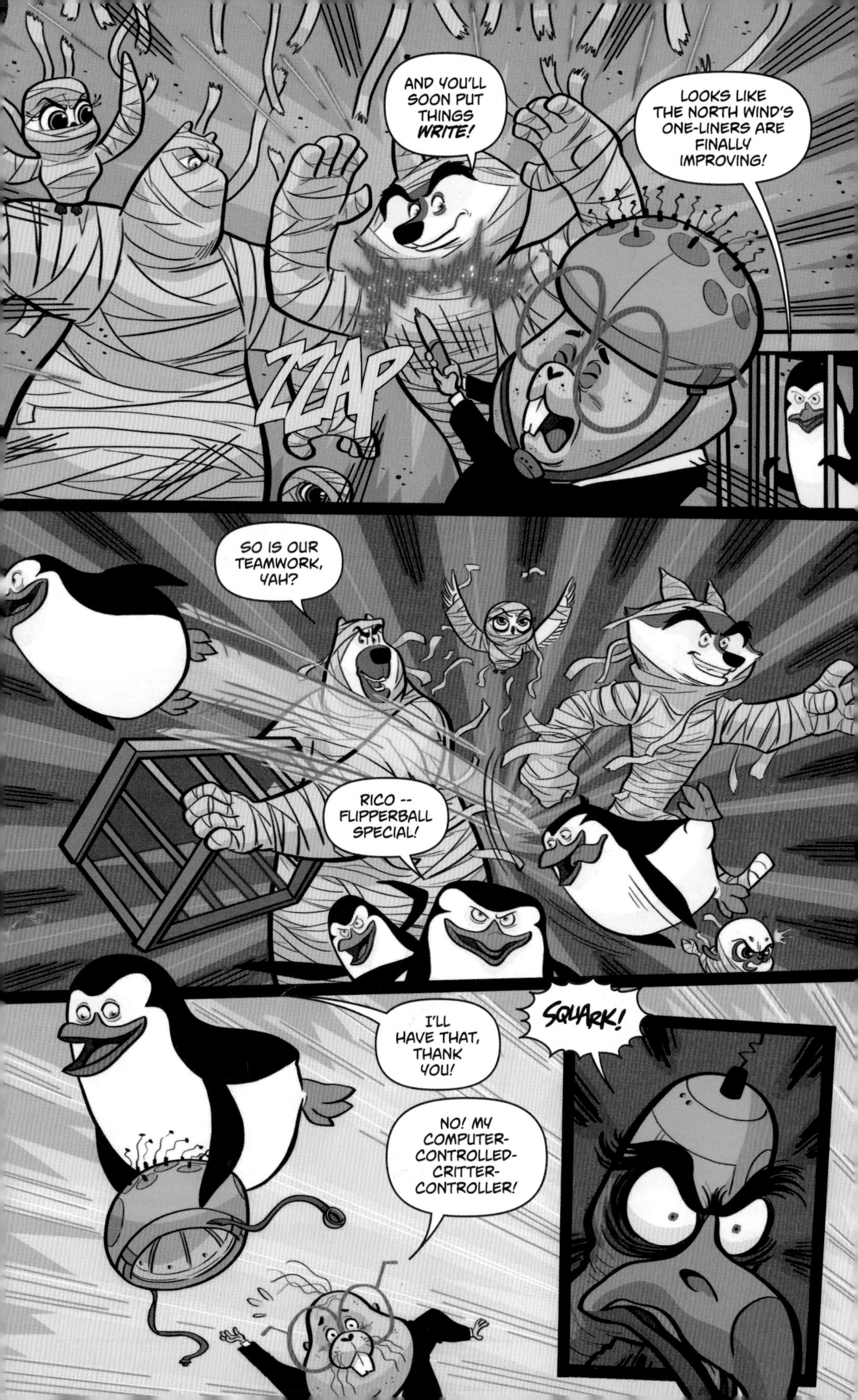
AND YOU'LL SOON PUT THINGS *WRITE!*
LOOKS LIKE THE NORTH WIND'S ONE-LINERS ARE FINALLY IMPROVING!
ZZAP
SO IS OUR TEAMWORK, YAH?
RICO -- FLIPPERBALL SPECIAL!
I'LL HAVE THAT, THANK YOU!
SQUARK!
NO! MY COMPUTER-CONTROLLED-CRITTER-CONTROLLER!

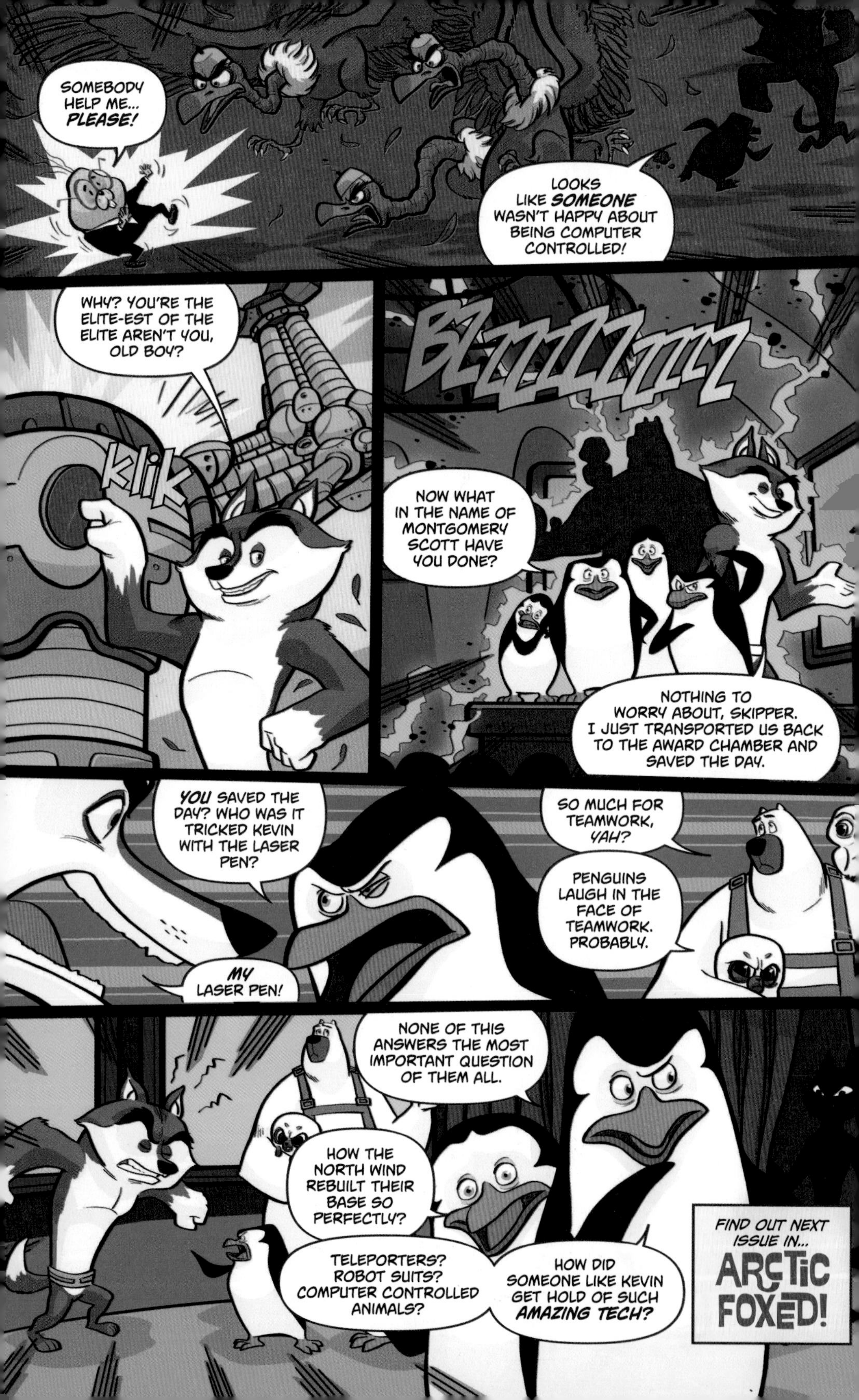
SOMEBODY HELP ME... PLEASE!
LOOKS LIKE SOMEONE WASN'T HAPPY ABOUT BEING COMPUTER CONTROLLED!
WHY? YOU'RE THE ELITE-EST OF THE ELITE AREN'T YOU, OLD BOY?
KLIK
BZZZZZZZZ
NOW WHAT IN THE NAME OF MONTGOMERY SCOTT HAVE YOU DONE?
NOTHING TO WORRY ABOUT, SKIPPER. I JUST TRANSPORTED US BACK TO THE AWARD CHAMBER AND SAVED THE DAY.
YOU SAVED THE DAY? WHO WAS IT TRICKED KEVIN WITH THE LASER PEN?
MY LASER PEN!
SO MUCH FOR TEAMWORK, YAH?
PENGUINS LAUGH IN THE FACE OF TEAMWORK. PROBABLY.
NONE OF THIS ANSWERS THE MOST IMPORTANT QUESTION OF THEM ALL.
HOW THE NORTH WIND REBUILT THEIR BASE SO PERFECTLY?
TELEPORTERS? ROBOT SUITS? COMPUTER CONTROLLED ANIMALS?
HOW DID SOMEONE LIKE KEVIN GET HOLD OF SUCH AMAZING TECH?
FIND OUT NEXT ISSUE IN... ARCTIC FOXED!

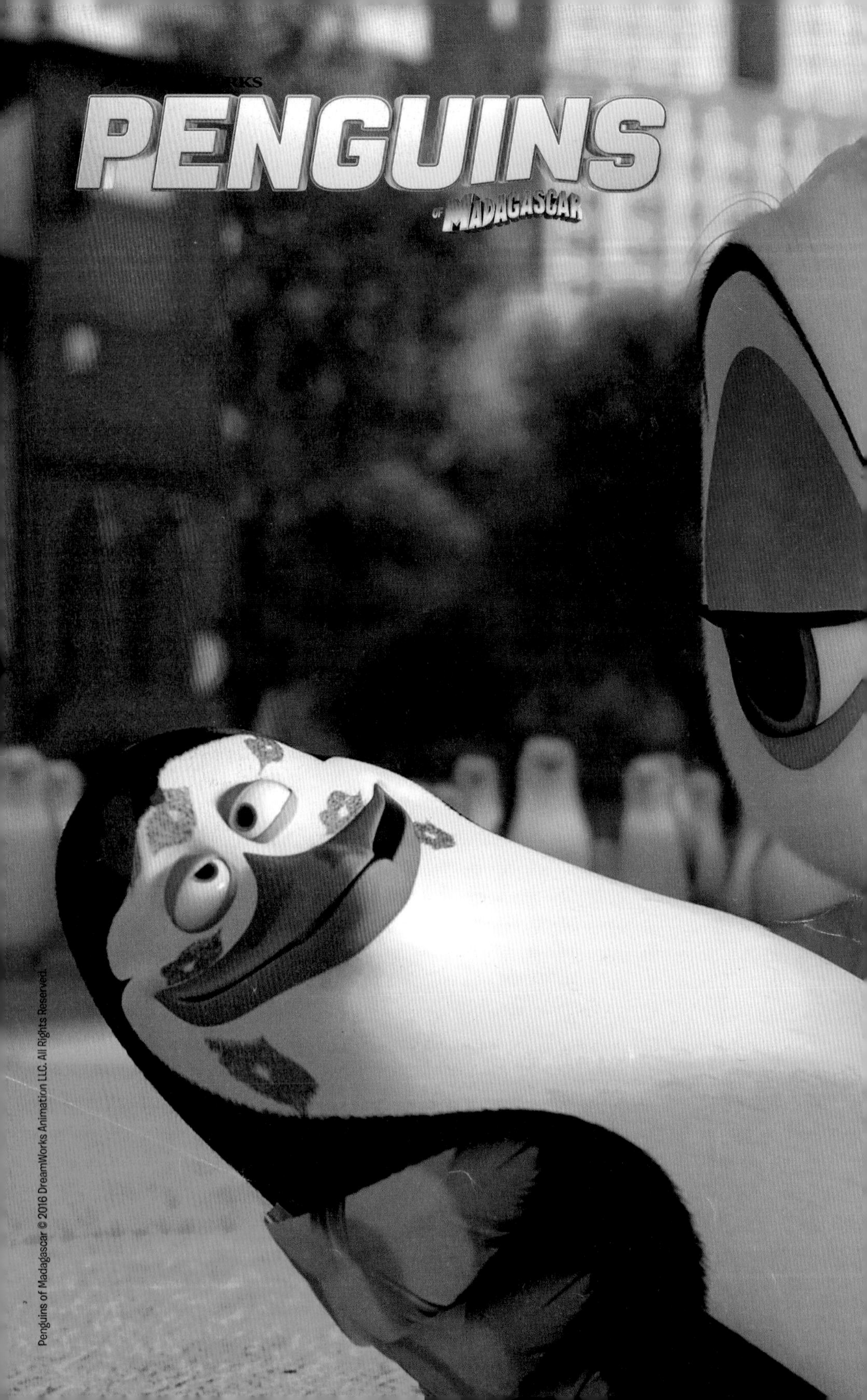
PENGUINS
OF MADAGASCAR

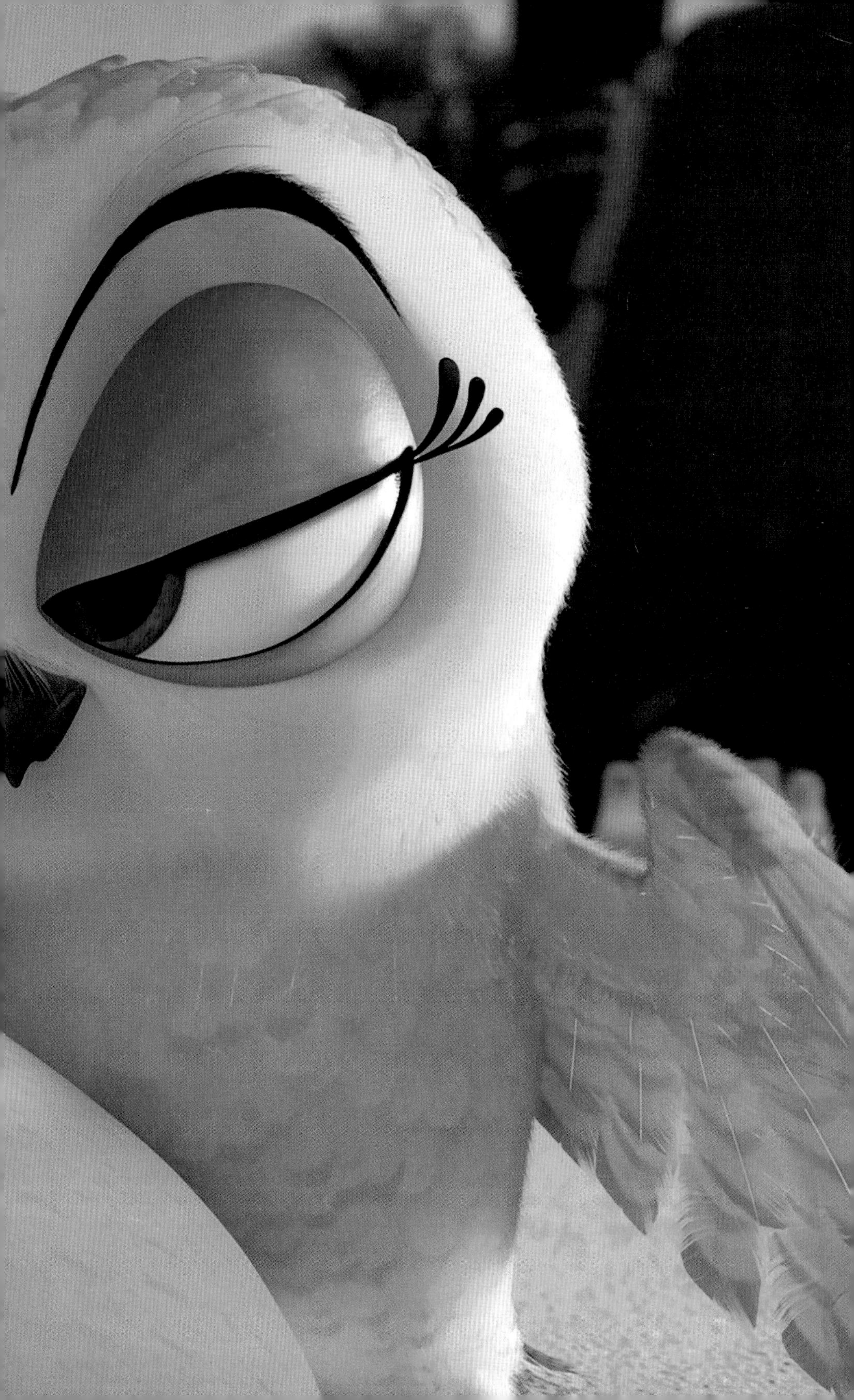

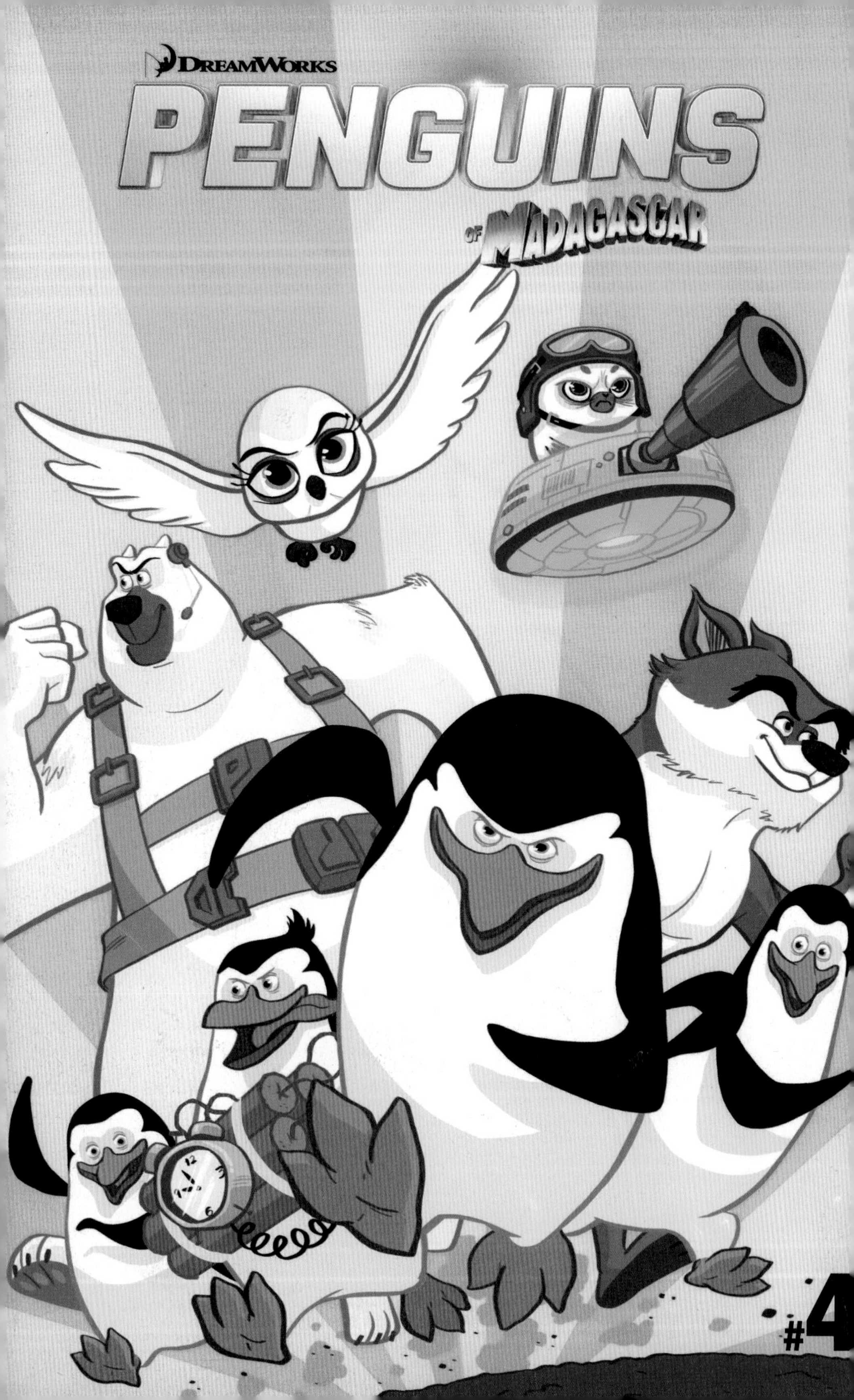
DreamWorks
PENGUINS
OF MADAGASCAR
#4

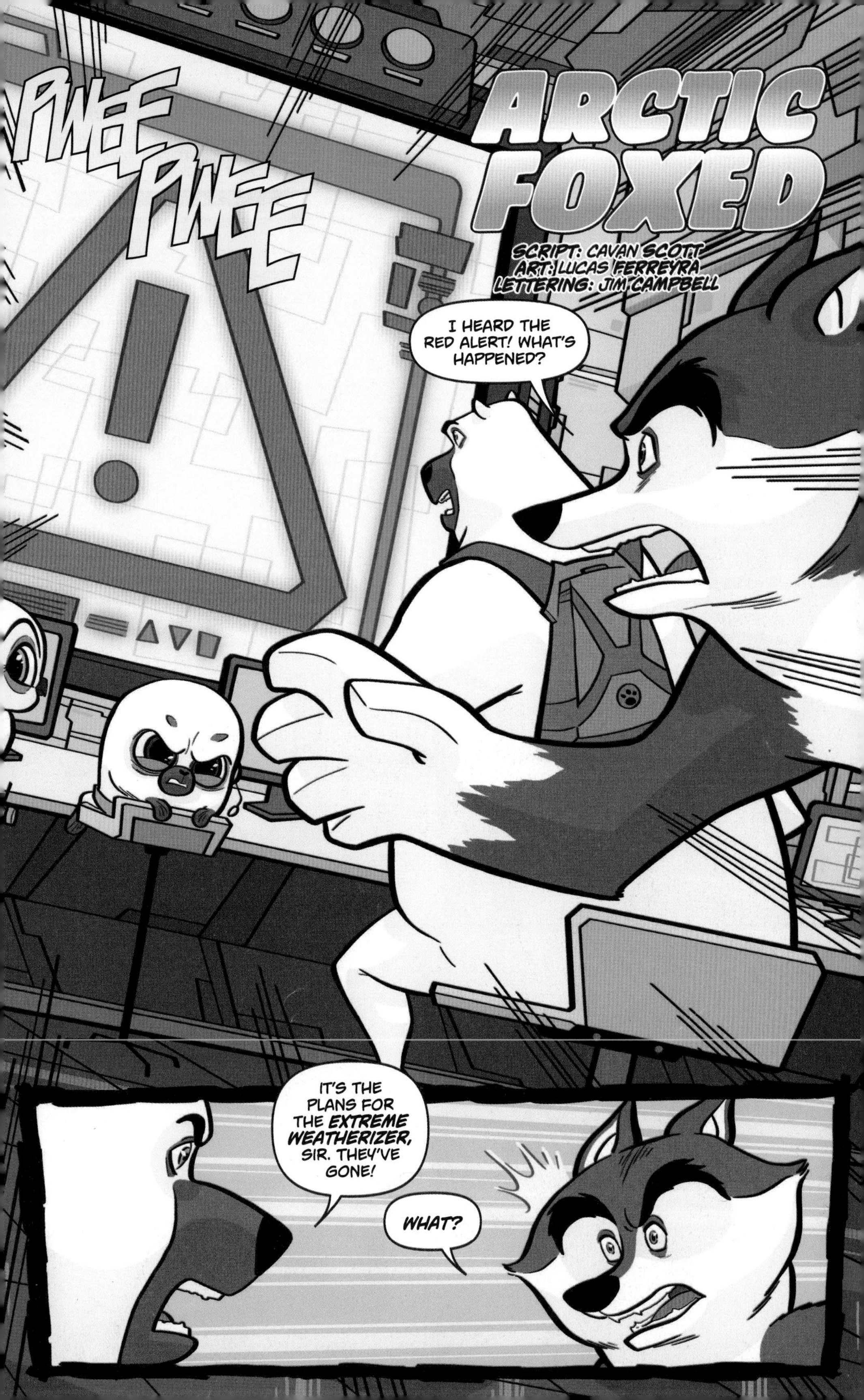
PWEE PWEE
ARCTIC FOXED
SCRIPT: CAVAN SCOTT
ART: LUCAS FERREYRA
LETTERING: JIM CAMPBELL
I HEARD THE RED ALERT! WHAT'S HAPPENED?
IT'S THE PLANS FOR THE EXTREME WEATHERIZER, SIR. THEY'VE GONE!
WHAT?

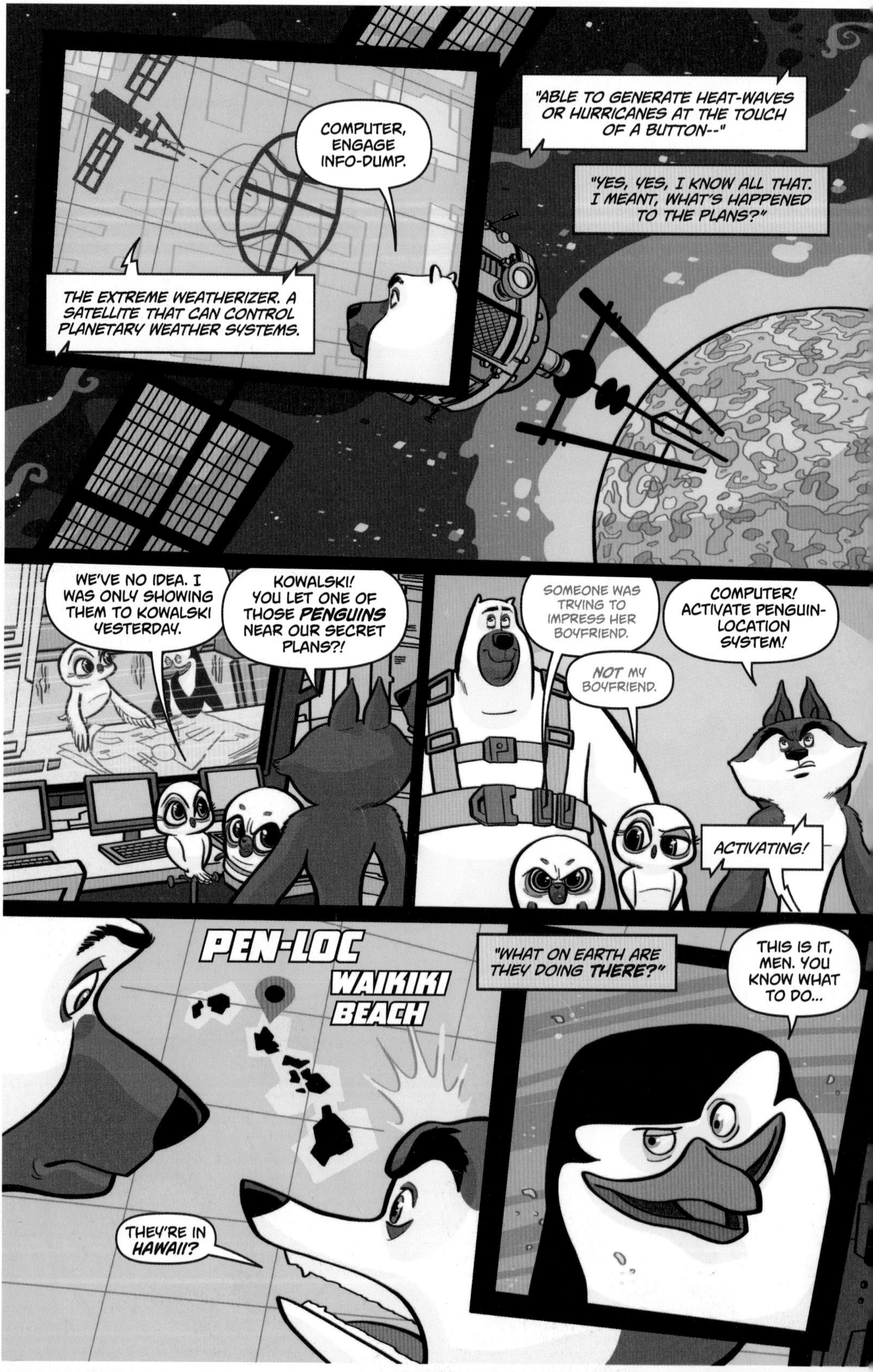
COMPUTER, ENGAGE INFO-DUMP.
THE EXTREME WEATHERIZER. A SATELLITE THAT CAN CONTROL PLANETARY WEATHER SYSTEMS.
"ABLE TO GENERATE HEAT-WAVES OR HURRICANES AT THE TOUCH OF A BUTTON--"
"YES, YES, I KNOW ALL THAT. I MEANT, WHAT'S HAPPENED TO THE PLANS?"
WE'VE NO IDEA. I WAS ONLY SHOWING THEM TO KOWALSKI YESTERDAY.
KOWALSKI! YOU LET ONE OF THOSE PENGUINS NEAR OUR SECRET PLANS?!
SOMEONE WAS TRYING TO IMPRESS HER BOYFRIEND.
NOT MY BOYFRIEND.
COMPUTER! ACTIVATE PENGUIN-LOCATION SYSTEM!
ACTIVATING!
PEN-LOC
WAIKIKI BEACH
"WHAT ON EARTH ARE THEY DOING THERE?"
THIS IS IT, MEN. YOU KNOW WHAT TO DO...
THEY'RE IN HAWAII?

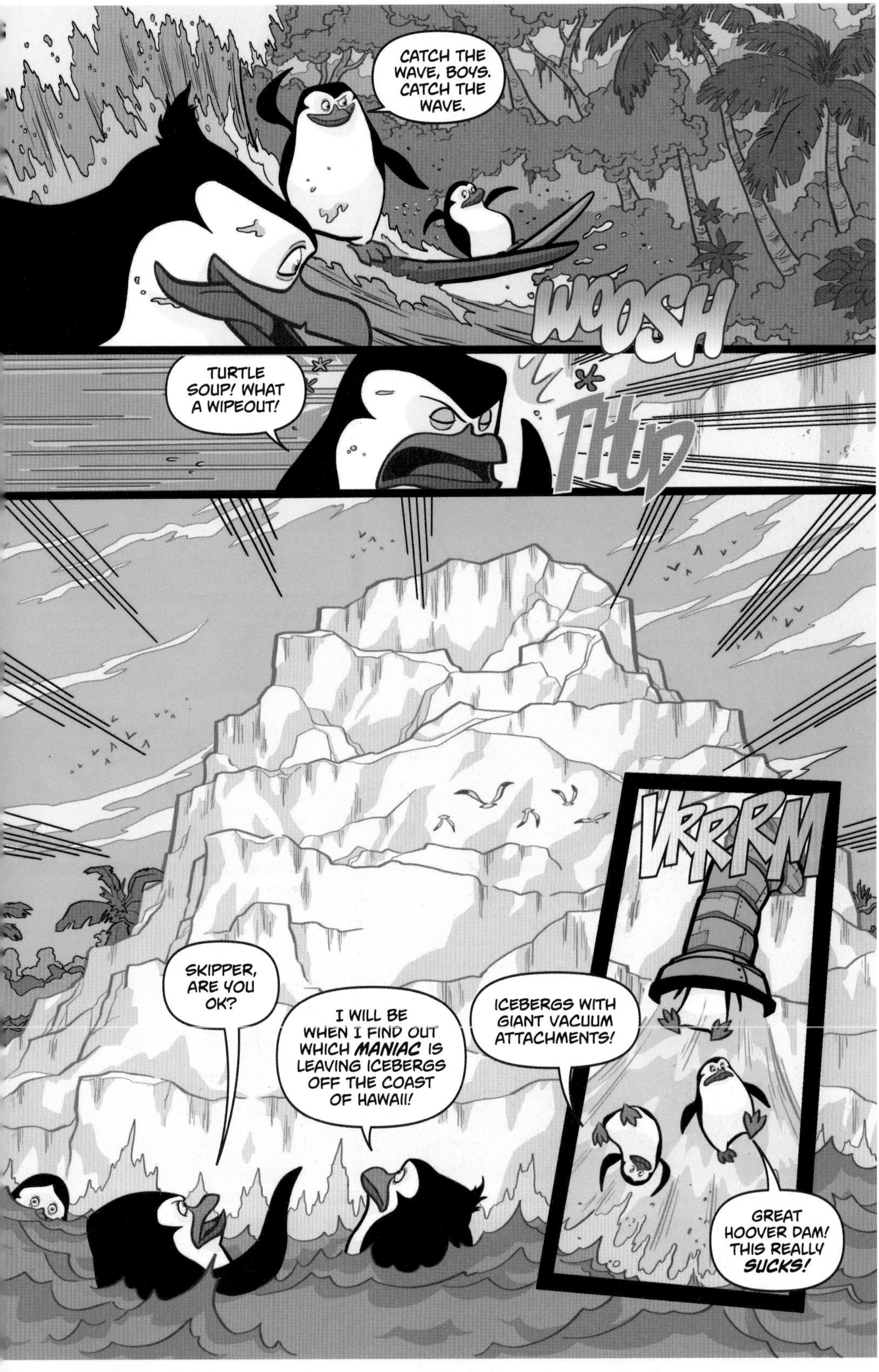

CATCH THE WAVE, BOYS. CATCH THE WAVE.
WOOSH
TURTLE SOUP! WHAT A WIPEOUT!
THUD
VRRRM
SKIPPER, ARE YOU OK?
I WILL BE WHEN I FIND OUT WHICH MANIAC IS LEAVING ICEBERGS OFF THE COAST OF HAWAII!
ICEBERGS WITH GIANT VACUUM ATTACHMENTS!
GREAT HOOVER DAM! THIS REALLY SUCKS!

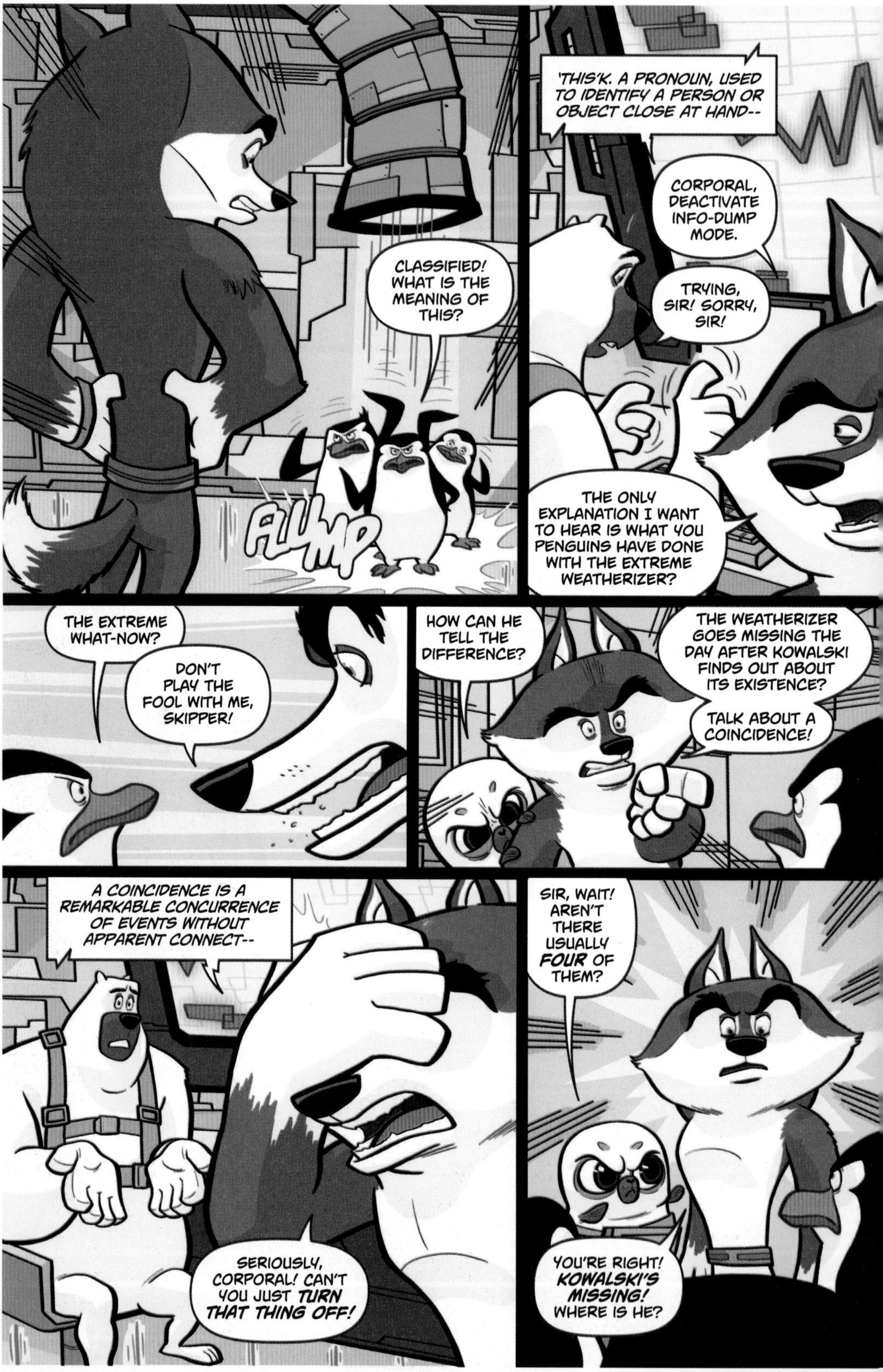
CLASSIFIED! WHAT IS THE MEANING OF THIS?
FLUMP
'THIS'K. A PRONOUN, USED TO IDENTIFY A PERSON OR OBJECT CLOSE AT HAND--
CORPORAL, DEACTIVATE INFO-DUMP MODE.
TRYING, SIR! SORRY, SIR!
THE ONLY EXPLANATION I WANT TO HEAR IS WHAT YOU PENGUINS HAVE DONE WITH THE EXTREME WEATHERIZER?
THE EXTREME WHAT-NOW?
DON'T PLAY THE FOOL WITH ME, SKIPPER!
HOW CAN HE TELL THE DIFFERENCE?
THE WEATHERIZER GOES MISSING THE DAY AFTER KOWALSKI FINDS OUT ABOUT ITS EXISTENCE?
TALK ABOUT A COINCIDENCE!
A COINCIDENCE IS A REMARKABLE CONCURRENCE OF EVENTS WITHOUT APPARENT CONNECT--
SERIOUSLY, CORPORAL! CAN'T YOU JUST TURN THAT THING OFF!
SIR, WAIT! AREN'T THERE USUALLY FOUR OF THEM?
YOU'RE RIGHT! KOWALSKI'S MISSING! WHERE IS HE?

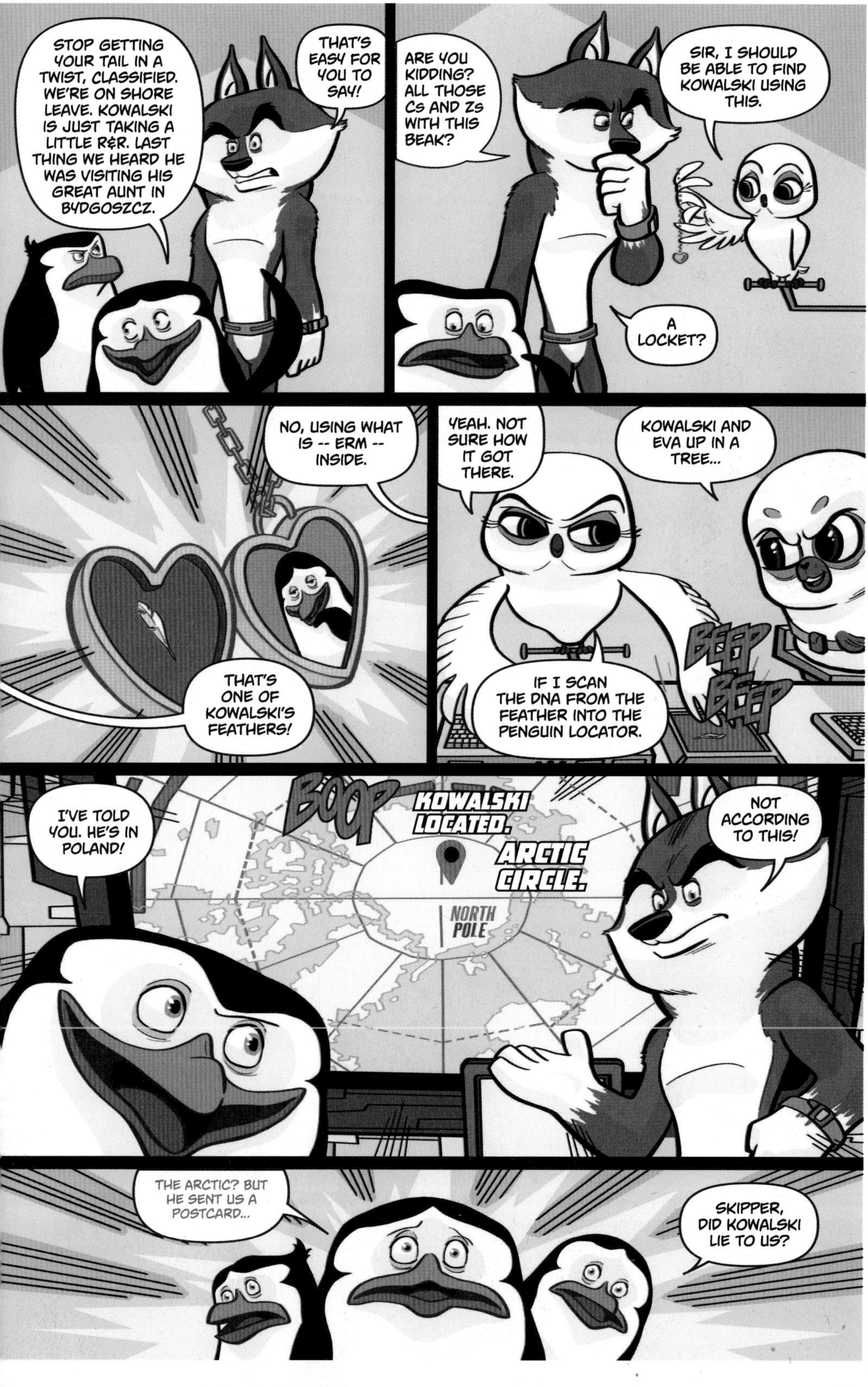
STOP GETTING YOUR TAIL IN A TWIST, CLASSIFIED. WE'RE ON SHORE LEAVE. KOWALSKI IS JUST TAKING A LITTLE R&R. LAST THING WE HEARD HE WAS VISITING HIS GREAT AUNT IN BYDGOSZCZ.
THAT'S EASY FOR YOU TO SAY!
ARE YOU KIDDING? ALL THOSE Cs AND Zs WITH THIS BEAK?
SIR, I SHOULD BE ABLE TO FIND KOWALSKI USING THIS.
A LOCKET?
NO, USING WHAT IS -- ERM -- INSIDE.
THAT'S ONE OF KOWALSKI'S FEATHERS!
YEAH. NOT SURE HOW IT GOT THERE.
KOWALSKI AND EVA UP IN A TREE...
IF I SCAN THE DNA FROM THE FEATHER INTO THE PENGUIN LOCATOR.
BEEP BEEP
I'VE TOLD YOU. HE'S IN POLAND!
BOOP
KOWALSKI LOCATED.
ARCTIC CIRCLE.
NORTH POLE
NOT ACCORDING TO THIS!
THE ARCTIC? BUT HE SENT US A POSTCARD...
SKIPPER, DID KOWALSKI LIE TO US?

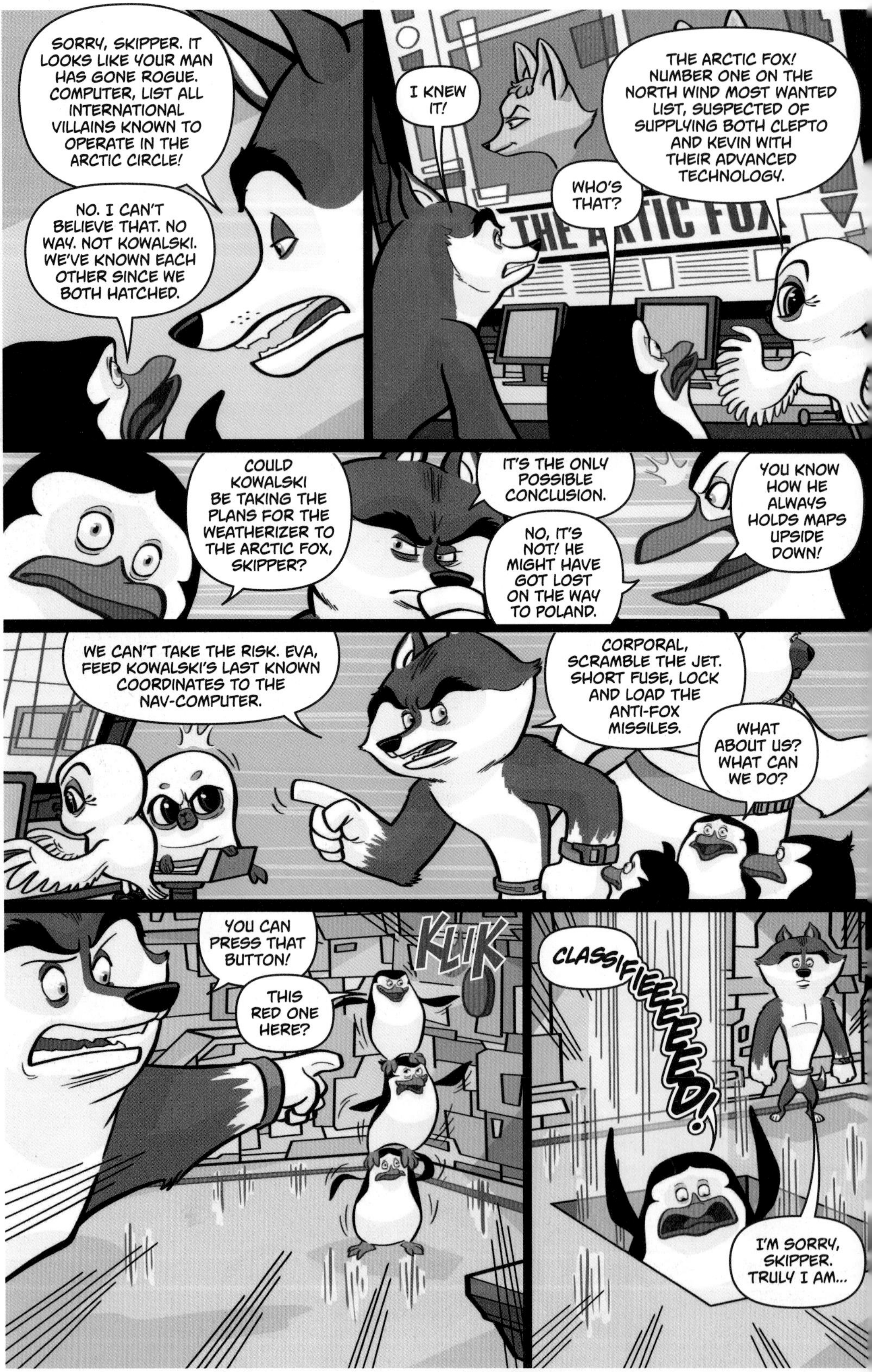
SORRY, SKIPPER. IT LOOKS LIKE YOUR MAN HAS GONE ROGUE. COMPUTER, LIST ALL INTERNATIONAL VILLAINS KNOWN TO OPERATE IN THE ARCTIC CIRCLE!
NO. I CAN'T BELIEVE THAT. NO WAY. NOT KOWALSKI. WE'VE KNOWN EACH OTHER SINCE WE BOTH HATCHED.
I KNEW IT!
WHO'S THAT?
THE ARCTIC FOX! NUMBER ONE ON THE NORTH WIND MOST WANTED LIST, SUSPECTED OF SUPPLYING BOTH CLEPTO AND KEVIN WITH THEIR ADVANCED TECHNOLOGY.
THE ARTIC FOX
COULD KOWALSKI BE TAKING THE PLANS FOR THE WEATHERIZER TO THE ARCTIC FOX, SKIPPER?
IT'S THE ONLY POSSIBLE CONCLUSION.
NO, IT'S NOT! HE MIGHT HAVE GOT LOST ON THE WAY TO POLAND.
YOU KNOW HOW HE ALWAYS HOLDS MAPS UPSIDE DOWN!
WE CAN'T TAKE THE RISK. EVA, FEED KOWALSKI'S LAST KNOWN COORDINATES TO THE NAV-COMPUTER.
CORPORAL, SCRAMBLE THE JET. SHORT FUSE, LOCK AND LOAD THE ANTI-FOX MISSILES.
WHAT ABOUT US? WHAT CAN WE DO?
YOU CAN PRESS THAT BUTTON!
THIS RED ONE HERE?
KLIK
CLASSIFIEEEEED!
I'M SORRY, SKIPPER. TRULY I AM...

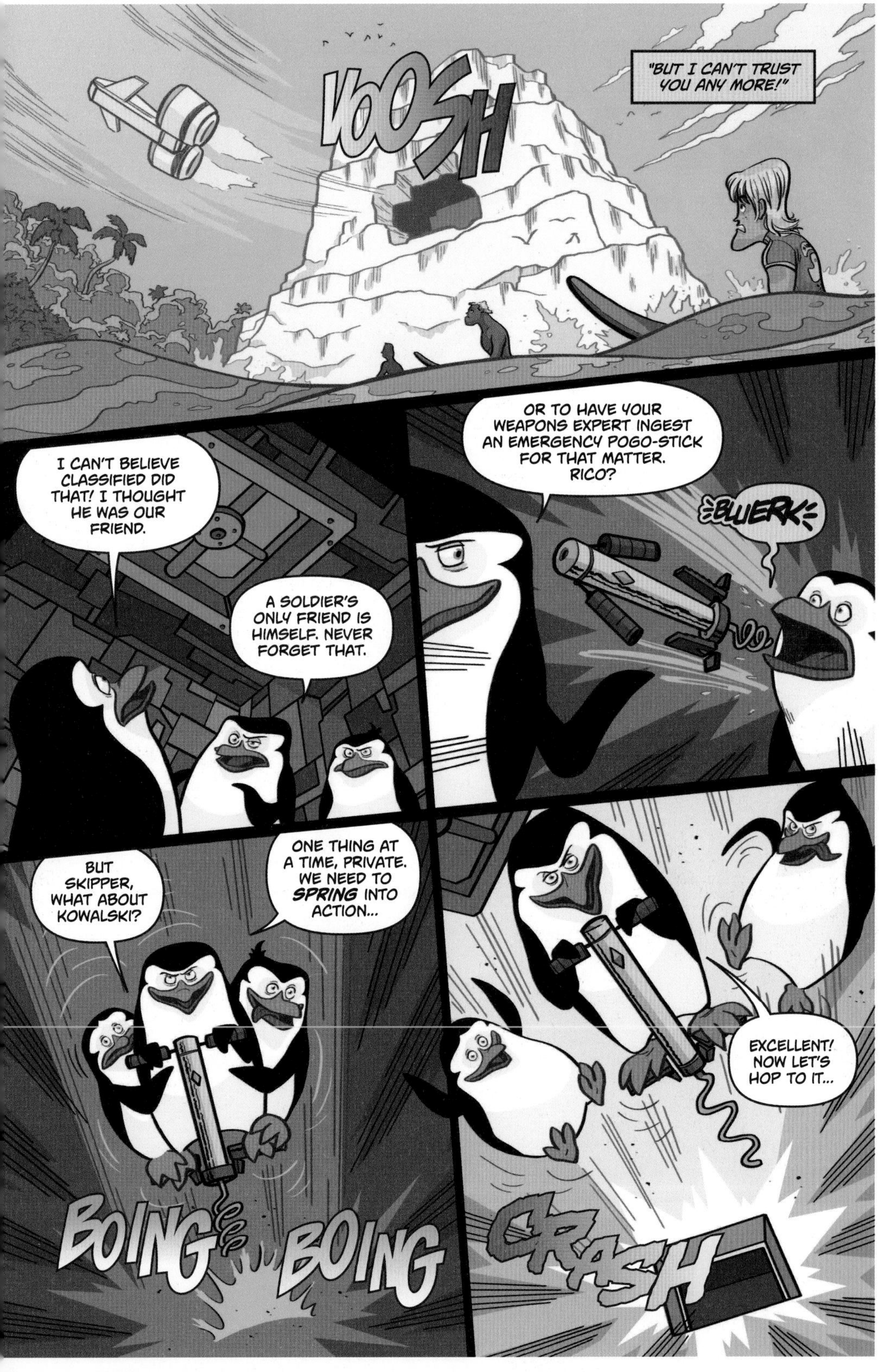

"BUT I CAN'T TRUST YOU ANY MORE!"
VOOSH
I CAN'T BELIEVE CLASSIFIED DID THAT! I THOUGHT HE WAS OUR FRIEND.
A SOLDIER'S ONLY FRIEND IS HIMSELF. NEVER FORGET THAT.
OR TO HAVE YOUR WEAPONS EXPERT INGEST AN EMERGENCY POGO-STICK FOR THAT MATTER. RICO?
BLUERK
BUT SKIPPER, WHAT ABOUT KOWALSKI?
ONE THING AT A TIME, PRIVATE. WE NEED TO *SPRING* INTO ACTION...
BOING
BOING
EXCELLENT! NOW LET'S HOP TO IT...
CRASH

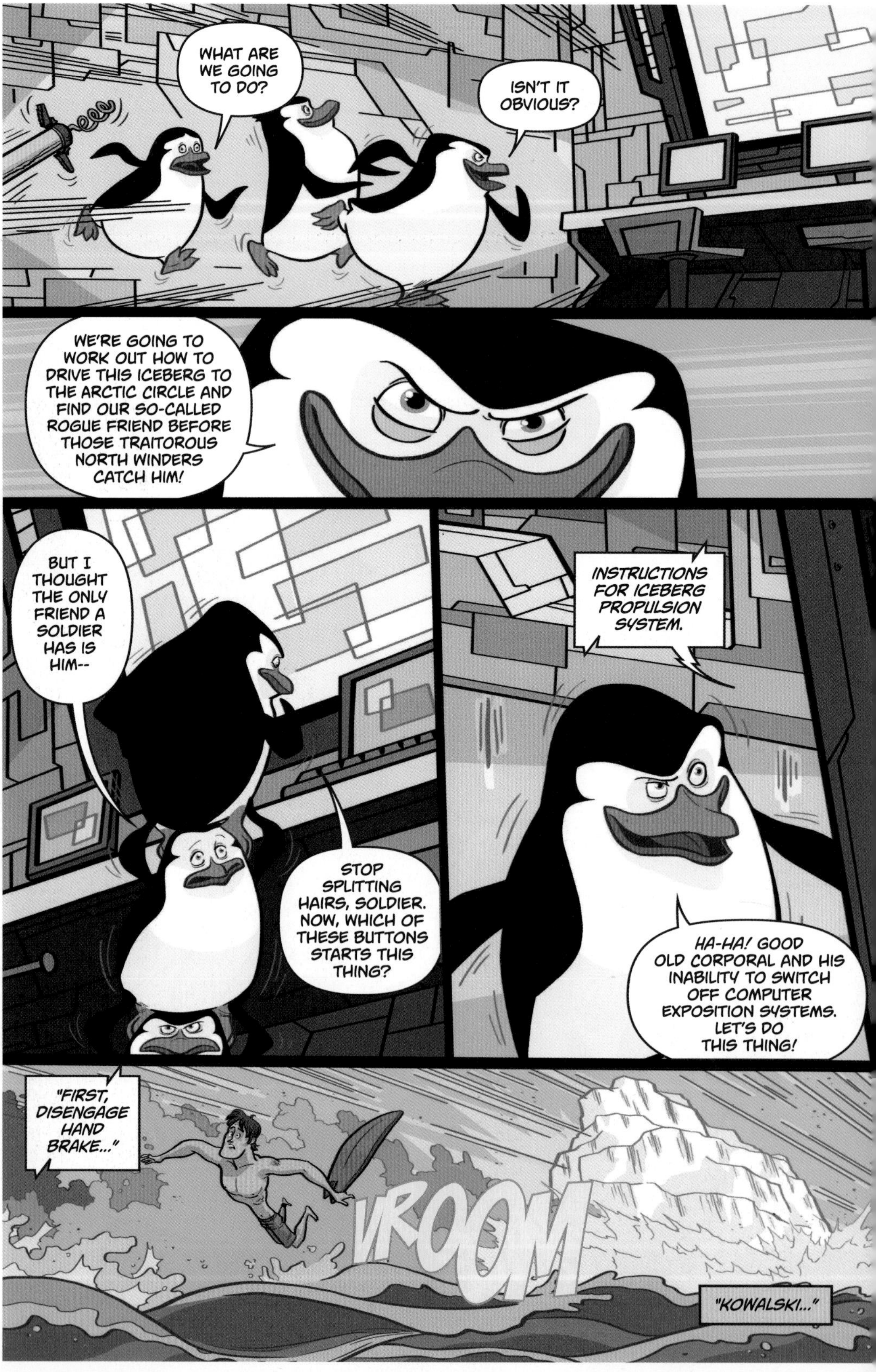
WHAT ARE WE GOING TO DO?
ISN'T IT OBVIOUS?
WE'RE GOING TO WORK OUT HOW TO DRIVE THIS ICEBERG TO THE ARCTIC CIRCLE AND FIND OUR SO-CALLED ROGUE FRIEND BEFORE THOSE TRAITOROUS NORTH WINDERS CATCH HIM!
BUT I THOUGHT THE ONLY FRIEND A SOLDIER HAS IS HIM--
STOP SPLITTING HAIRS, SOLDIER. NOW, WHICH OF THESE BUTTONS STARTS THIS THING?
INSTRUCTIONS FOR ICEBERG PROPULSION SYSTEM.
HA-HA! GOOD OLD CORPORAL AND HIS INABILITY TO SWITCH OFF COMPUTER EXPOSITION SYSTEMS. LET'S DO THIS THING!
"FIRST, DISENGAGE HAND BRAKE..."
VROOM
"KOWALSKI..."

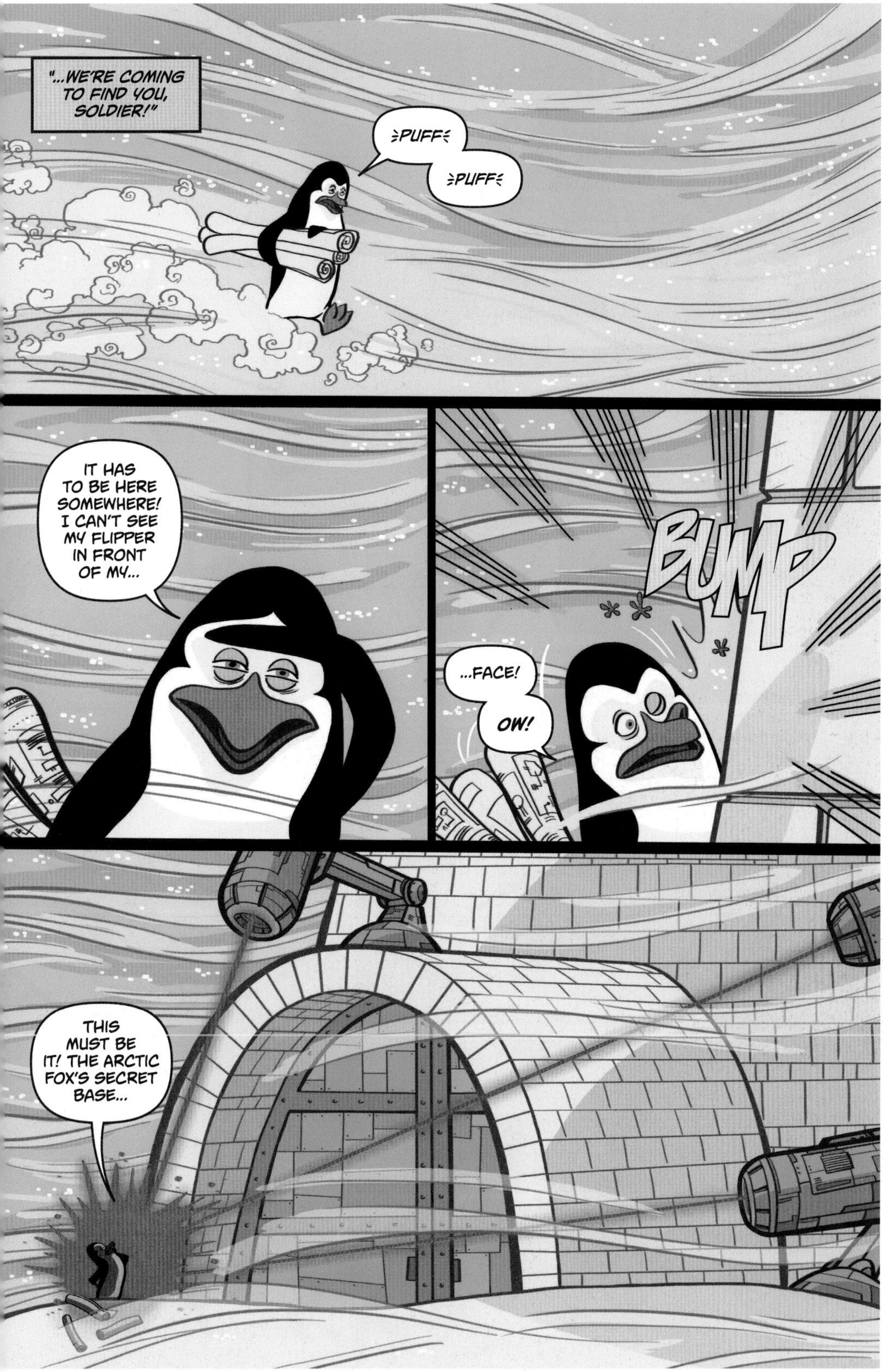
"...WE'RE COMING TO FIND YOU, SOLDIER!"
PUFF
PUFF
IT HAS TO BE HERE SOMEWHERE! I CAN'T SEE MY FLIPPER IN FRONT OF MY...
BUMP
...FACE!
OW!
THIS MUST BE IT! THE ARCTIC FOX'S SECRET BASE...

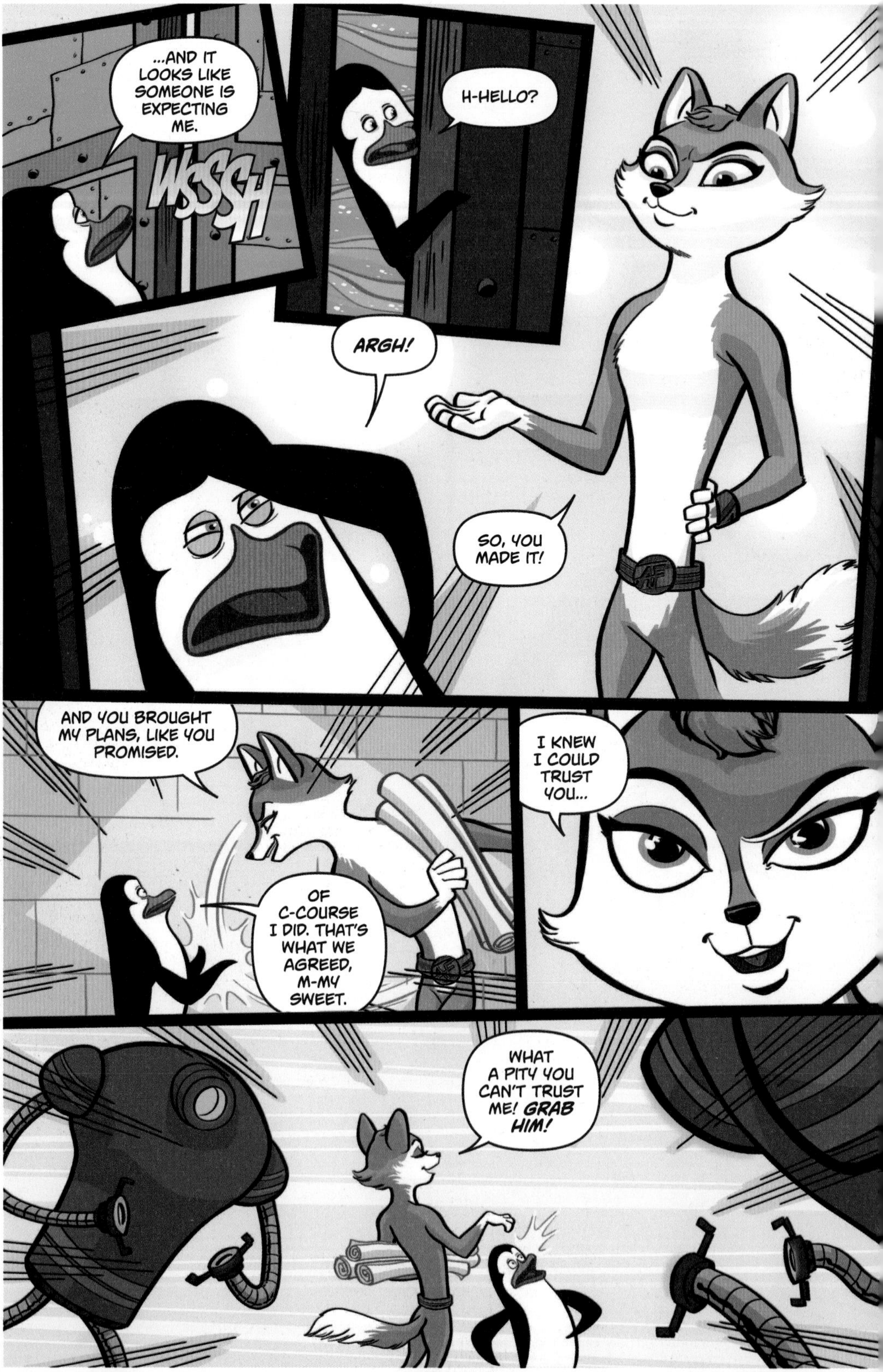
...AND IT LOOKS LIKE SOMEONE IS EXPECTING ME.
WSSSH
H-HELLO?
ARGH!
SO, YOU MADE IT!
AND YOU BROUGHT MY PLANS, LIKE YOU PROMISED.
OF C-COURSE I DID. THAT'S WHAT WE AGREED, M-MY SWEET.
I KNEW I COULD TRUST YOU...
WHAT A PITY YOU CAN'T TRUST ME! GRAB HIM!

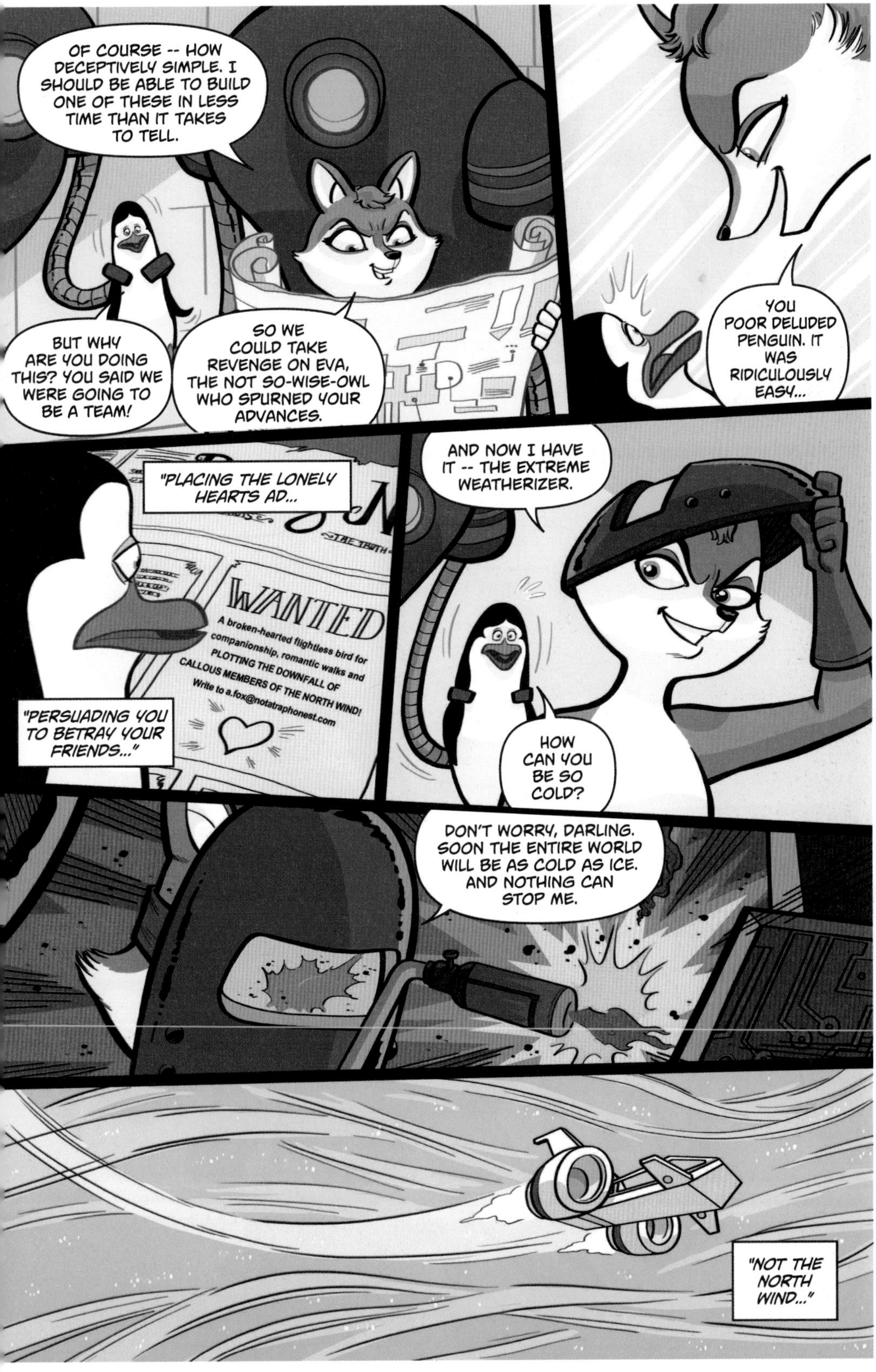
OF COURSE -- HOW DECEPTIVELY SIMPLE. I SHOULD BE ABLE TO BUILD ONE OF THESE IN LESS TIME THAN IT TAKES TO TELL.
BUT WHY ARE YOU DOING THIS? YOU SAID WE WERE GOING TO BE A TEAM!
SO WE COULD TAKE REVENGE ON EVA, THE NOT SO-WISE-OWL WHO SPURNED YOUR ADVANCES.
YOU POOR DELUDED PENGUIN. IT WAS RIDICULOUSLY EASY...
"PLACING THE LONELY HEARTS AD...
WANTED
A broken-hearted flightless bird for companionship, romantic walks and PLOTTING THE DOWNFALL OF CALLOUS MEMBERS OF THE NORTH WIND!
Write to a.fox@notatraphonest.com
"PERSUADING YOU TO BETRAY YOUR FRIENDS..."
AND NOW I HAVE IT -- THE EXTREME WEATHERIZER.
HOW CAN YOU BE SO COLD?
DON'T WORRY, DARLING. SOON THE ENTIRE WORLD WILL BE AS COLD AS ICE. AND NOTHING CAN STOP ME.
"NOT THE NORTH WIND..."

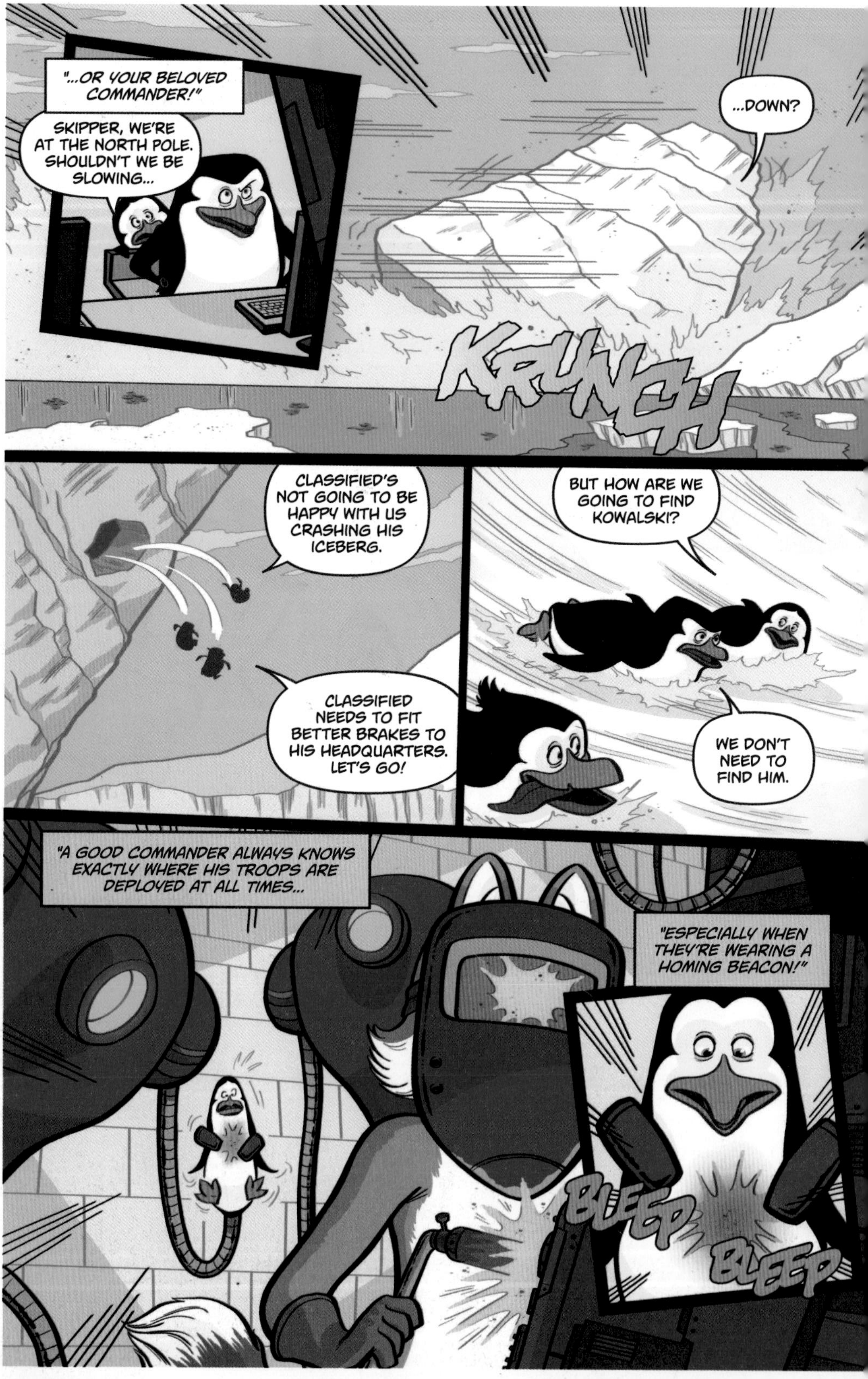
"...OR YOUR BELOVED COMMANDER!"
SKIPPER, WE'RE AT THE NORTH POLE. SHOULDN'T WE BE SLOWING...
...DOWN?
KRUNCH
CLASSIFIED'S NOT GOING TO BE HAPPY WITH US CRASHING HIS ICEBERG.
CLASSIFIED NEEDS TO FIT BETTER BRAKES TO HIS HEADQUARTERS. LET'S GO!
BUT HOW ARE WE GOING TO FIND KOWALSKI?
WE DON'T NEED TO FIND HIM.
"A GOOD COMMANDER ALWAYS KNOWS EXACTLY WHERE HIS TROOPS ARE DEPLOYED AT ALL TIMES...
"ESPECIALLY WHEN THEY'RE WEARING A HOMING BEACON!"
BLEEP
BLEEP

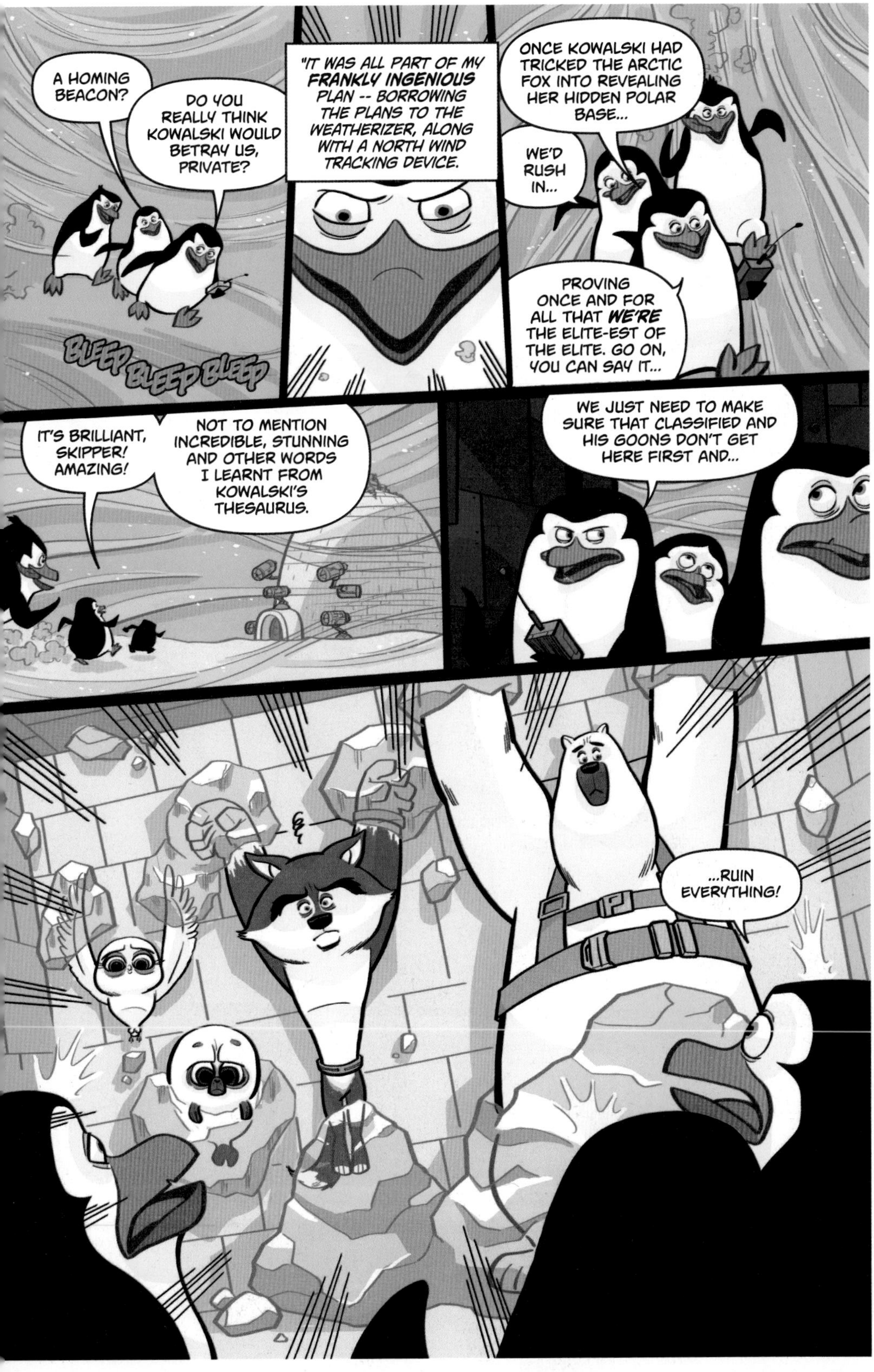
A HOMING BEACON?
DO YOU REALLY THINK KOWALSKI WOULD BETRAY US, PRIVATE?
BLEEP BLEEP BLEEP
"IT WAS ALL PART OF MY *FRANKLY INGENIOUS* PLAN -- BORROWING THE PLANS TO THE WEATHERIZER, ALONG WITH A NORTH WIND TRACKING DEVICE.
ONCE KOWALSKI HAD TRICKED THE ARCTIC FOX INTO REVEALING HER HIDDEN POLAR BASE...
WE'D RUSH IN...
PROVING ONCE AND FOR ALL THAT ***WE'RE*** THE ELITE-EST OF THE ELITE. GO ON, YOU CAN SAY IT...
IT'S BRILLIANT, SKIPPER! AMAZING!
NOT TO MENTION INCREDIBLE, STUNNING AND OTHER WORDS I LEARNT FROM KOWALSKI'S THESAURUS.
WE JUST NEED TO MAKE SURE THAT CLASSIFIED AND HIS GOONS DON'T GET HERE FIRST AND...
...RUIN EVERYTHING!

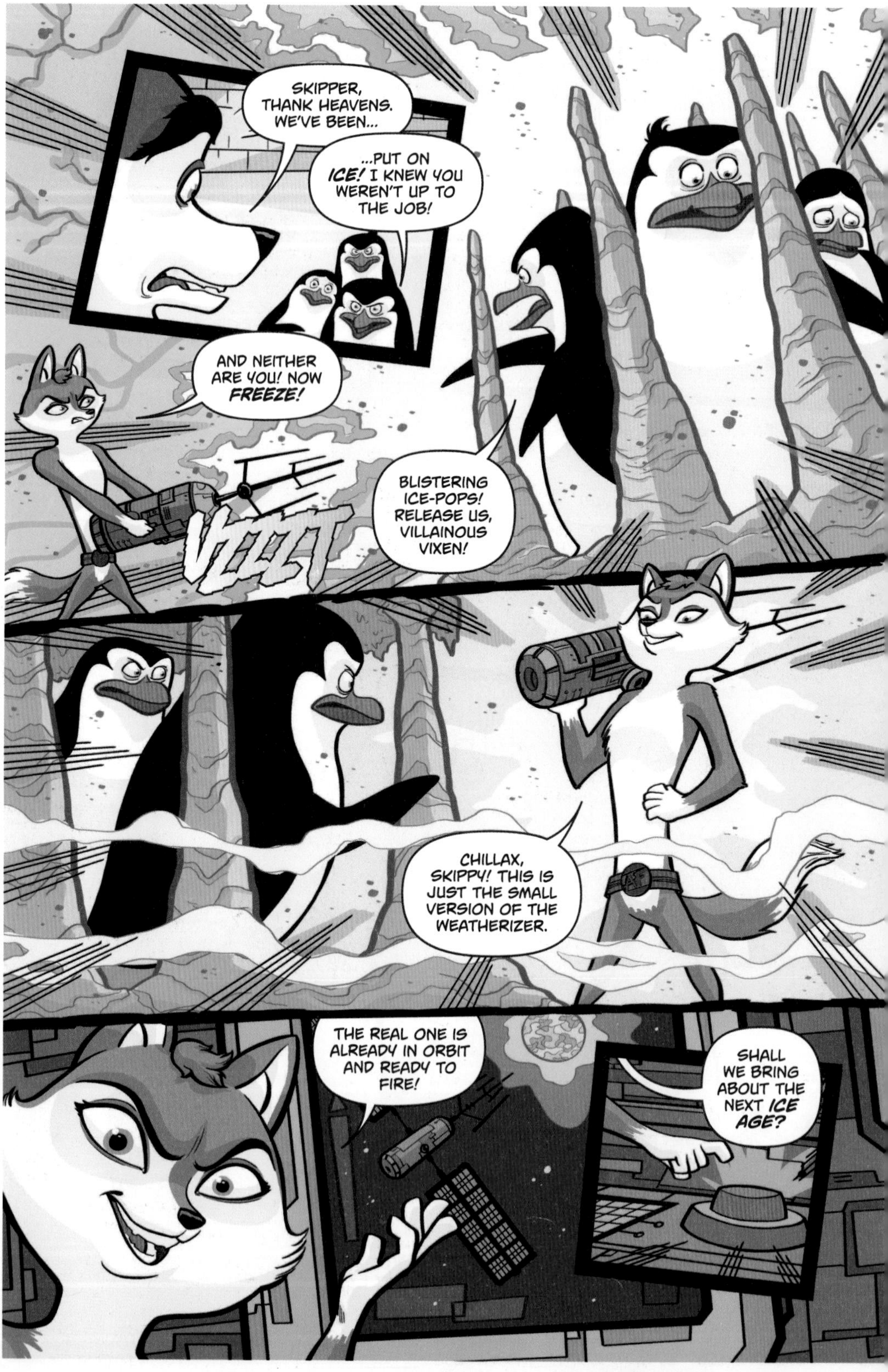
SKIPPER, THANK HEAVENS. WE'VE BEEN...
...PUT ON ICE! I KNEW YOU WEREN'T UP TO THE JOB!
AND NEITHER ARE YOU! NOW FREEZE!
VZZZT
BLISTERING ICE-POPS! RELEASE US, VILLAINOUS VIXEN!
CHILLAX, SKIPPY! THIS IS JUST THE SMALL VERSION OF THE WEATHERIZER.
THE REAL ONE IS ALREADY IN ORBIT AND READY TO FIRE!
SHALL WE BRING ABOUT THE NEXT ICE AGE?

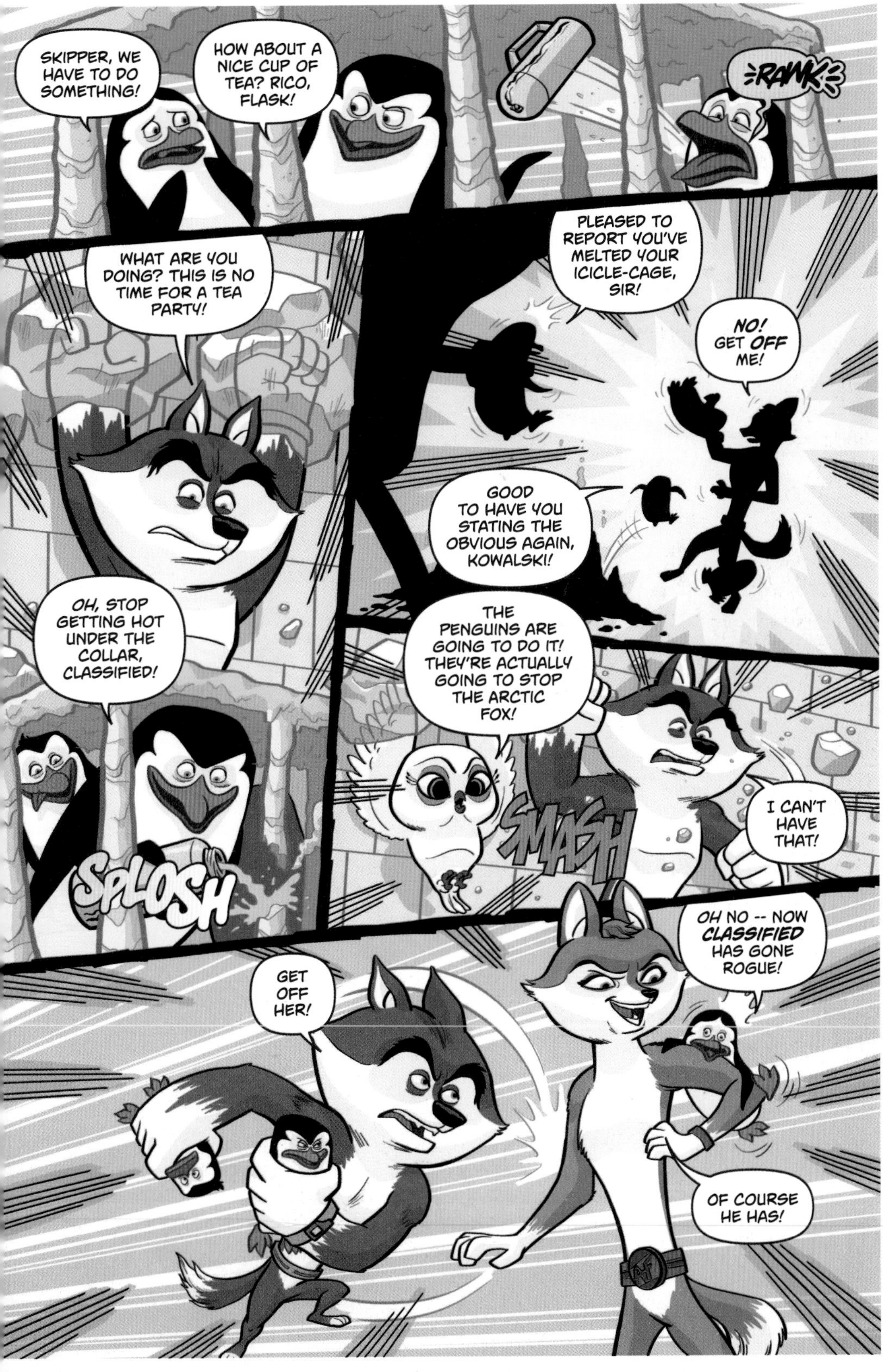
SKIPPER, WE HAVE TO DO SOMETHING!
HOW ABOUT A NICE CUP OF TEA? RICO, FLASK!
RAWK
WHAT ARE YOU DOING? THIS IS NO TIME FOR A TEA PARTY!
OH, STOP GETTING HOT UNDER THE COLLAR, CLASSIFIED!
SPLOSH
PLEASED TO REPORT YOU'VE MELTED YOUR ICICLE-CAGE, SIR!
NO! GET OFF ME!
GOOD TO HAVE YOU STATING THE OBVIOUS AGAIN, KOWALSKI!
THE PENGUINS ARE GOING TO DO IT! THEY'RE ACTUALLY GOING TO STOP THE ARCTIC FOX!
SMASH
I CAN'T HAVE THAT!
GET OFF HER!
OH NO -- NOW CLASSIFIED HAS GONE ROGUE!
OF COURSE HE HAS!

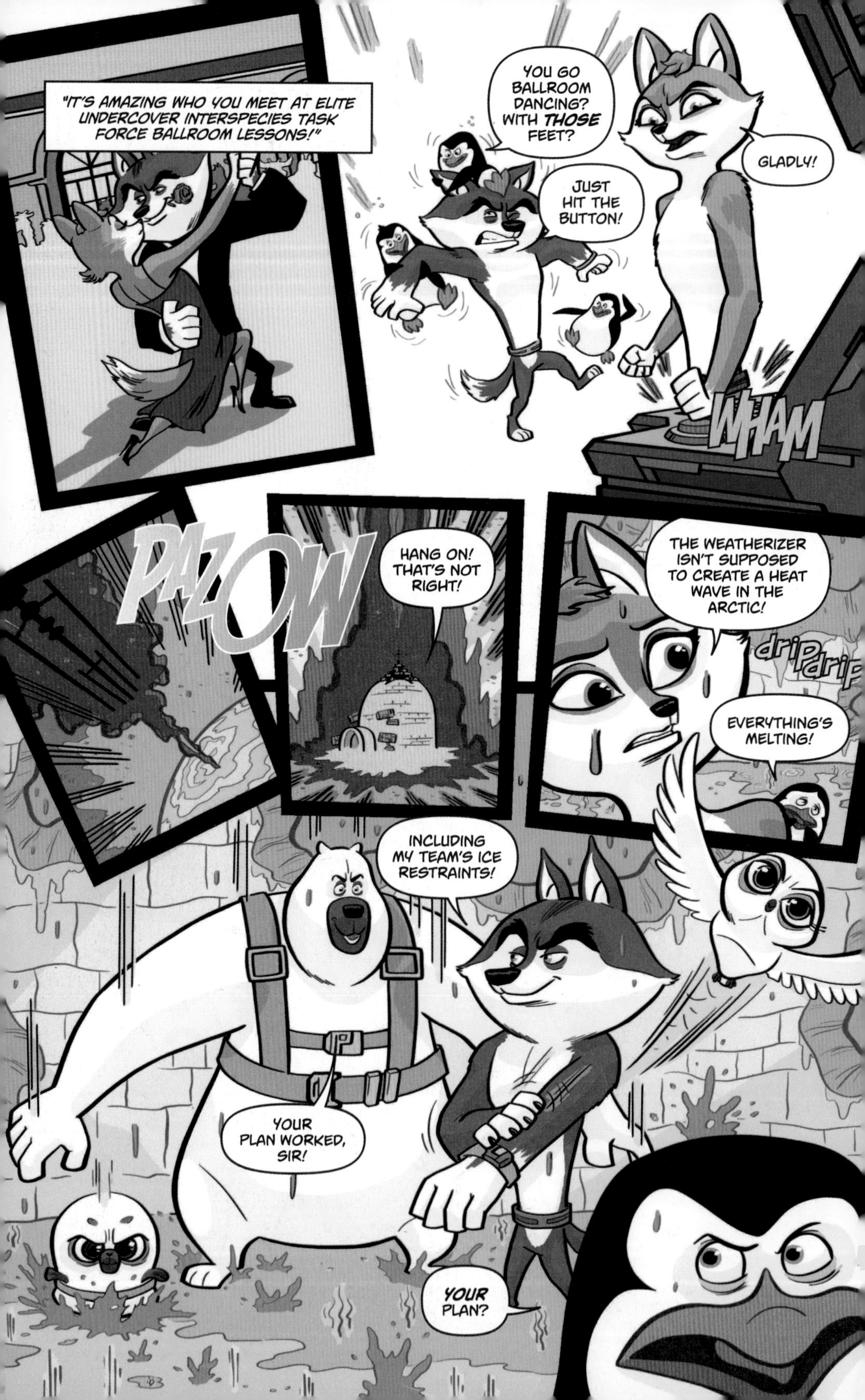
"IT'S AMAZING WHO YOU MEET AT ELITE UNDERCOVER INTERSPECIES TASK FORCE BALLROOM LESSONS!"
YOU GO BALLROOM DANCING? WITH THOSE FEET?
JUST HIT THE BUTTON!
GLADLY!
WHAM
PAZOW
HANG ON! THAT'S NOT RIGHT!
THE WEATHERIZER ISN'T SUPPOSED TO CREATE A HEAT WAVE IN THE ARCTIC!
drip drip
EVERYTHING'S MELTING!
INCLUDING MY TEAM'S ICE RESTRAINTS!
YOUR PLAN WORKED, SIR!
YOUR PLAN?

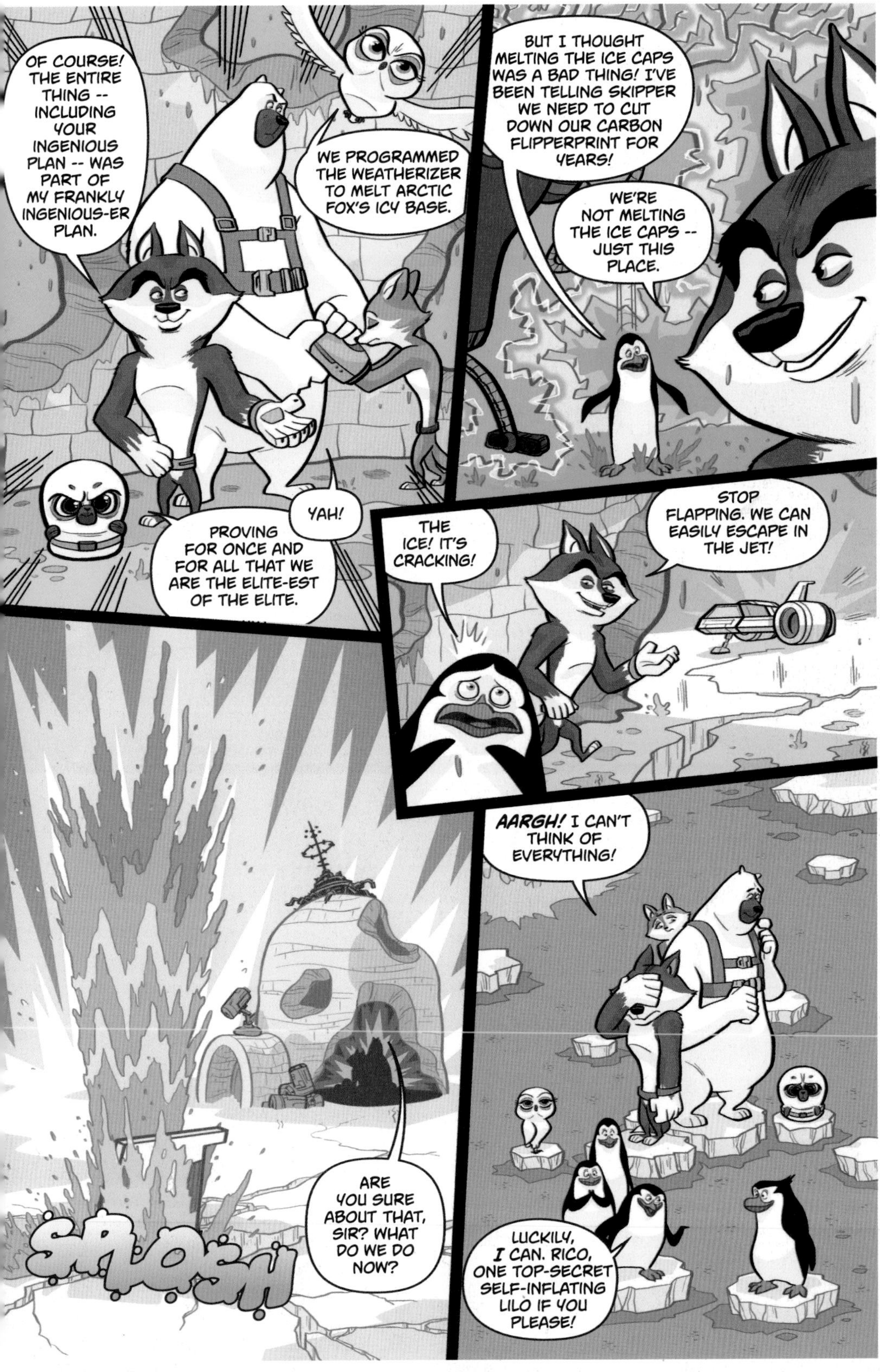
OF COURSE! THE ENTIRE THING -- INCLUDING YOUR INGENIOUS PLAN -- WAS PART OF MY FRANKLY INGENIOUS-ER PLAN.
WE PROGRAMMED THE WEATHERIZER TO MELT ARCTIC FOX'S ICY BASE.
PROVING FOR ONCE AND FOR ALL THAT WE ARE THE ELITE-EST OF THE ELITE.
YAH!
BUT I THOUGHT MELTING THE ICE CAPS WAS A BAD THING! I'VE BEEN TELLING SKIPPER WE NEED TO CUT DOWN OUR CARBON FLIPPERPRINT FOR YEARS!
WE'RE NOT MELTING THE ICE CAPS -- JUST THIS PLACE.
THE ICE! IT'S CRACKING!
STOP FLAPPING. WE CAN EASILY ESCAPE IN THE JET!
SPLOOSH
ARE YOU SURE ABOUT THAT, SIR? WHAT DO WE DO NOW?
AARGH! I CAN'T THINK OF EVERYTHING!
LUCKILY, I CAN. RICO, ONE TOP-SECRET SELF-INFLATING LILO IF YOU PLEASE!

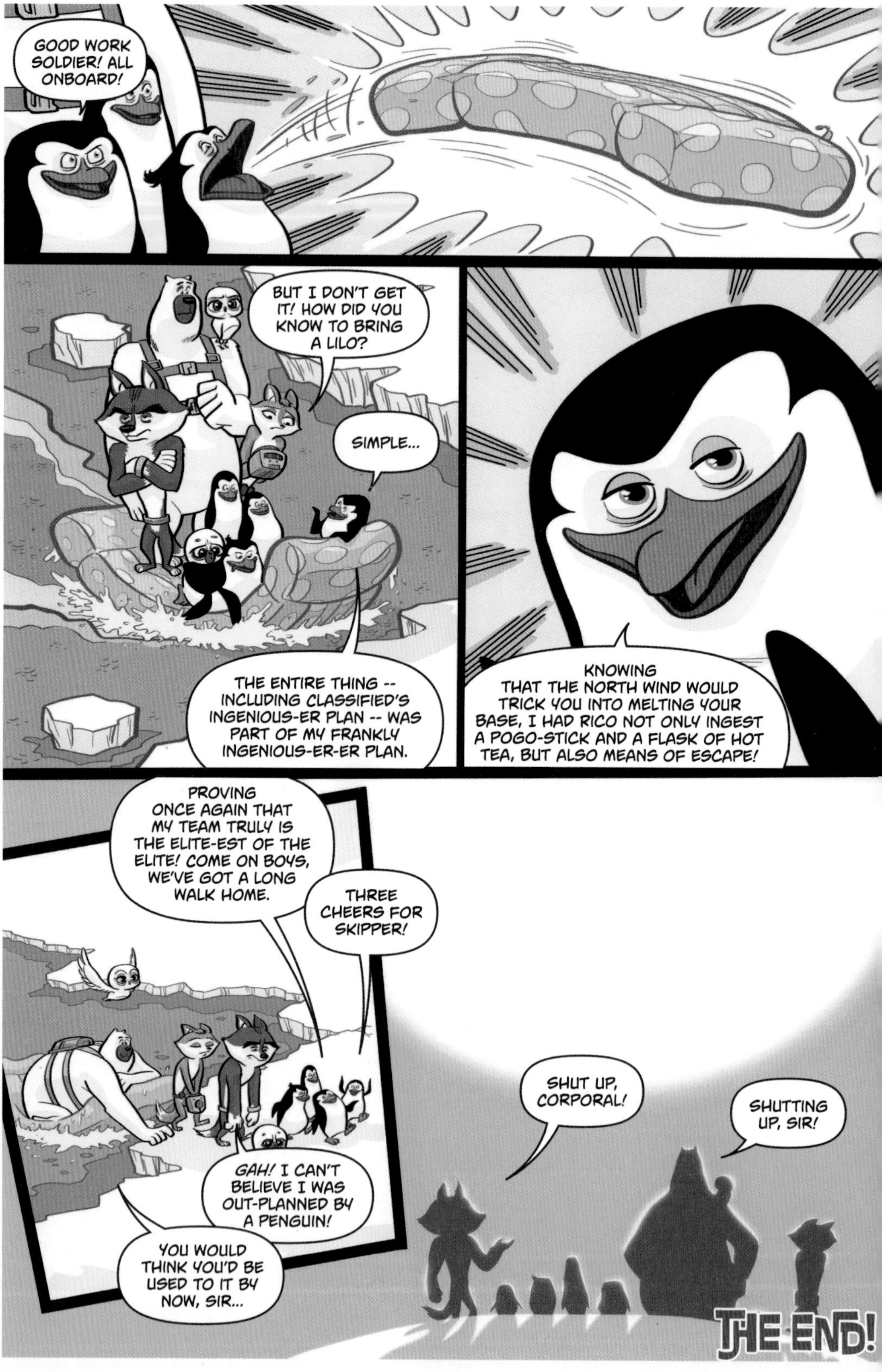
GOOD WORK SOLDIER! ALL ONBOARD!
BUT I DON'T GET IT! HOW DID YOU KNOW TO BRING A LILO?
SIMPLE...
THE ENTIRE THING -- INCLUDING CLASSIFIED'S INGENIOUS-ER PLAN -- WAS PART OF MY FRANKLY INGENIOUS-ER-ER PLAN.
KNOWING THAT THE NORTH WIND WOULD TRICK YOU INTO MELTING YOUR BASE, I HAD RICO NOT ONLY INGEST A POGO-STICK AND A FLASK OF HOT TEA, BUT ALSO MEANS OF ESCAPE!
PROVING ONCE AGAIN THAT MY TEAM TRULY IS THE ELITE-EST OF THE ELITE! COME ON BOYS, WE'VE GOT A LONG WALK HOME.
THREE CHEERS FOR SKIPPER!
GAH! I CAN'T BELIEVE I WAS OUT-PLANNED BY A PENGUIN!
YOU WOULD THINK YOU'D BE USED TO IT BY NOW, SIR...
SHUT UP, CORPORAL!
SHUTTING UP, SIR!
THE END!

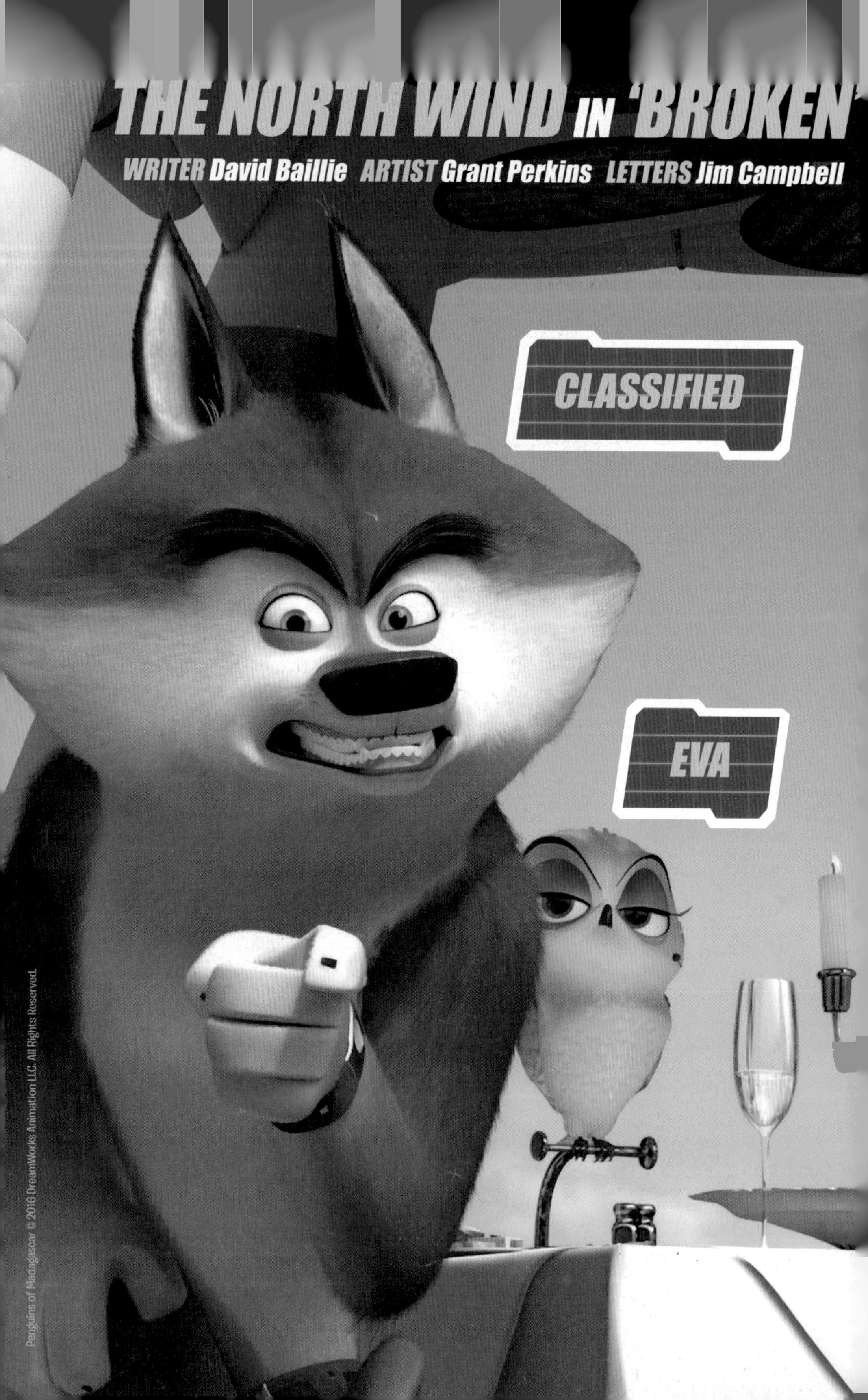
THE NORTH WIND IN 'BROKEN'
WRITER David Baillie ARTIST Grant Perkins LETTERS Jim Campbell
CLASSIFIED
EVA

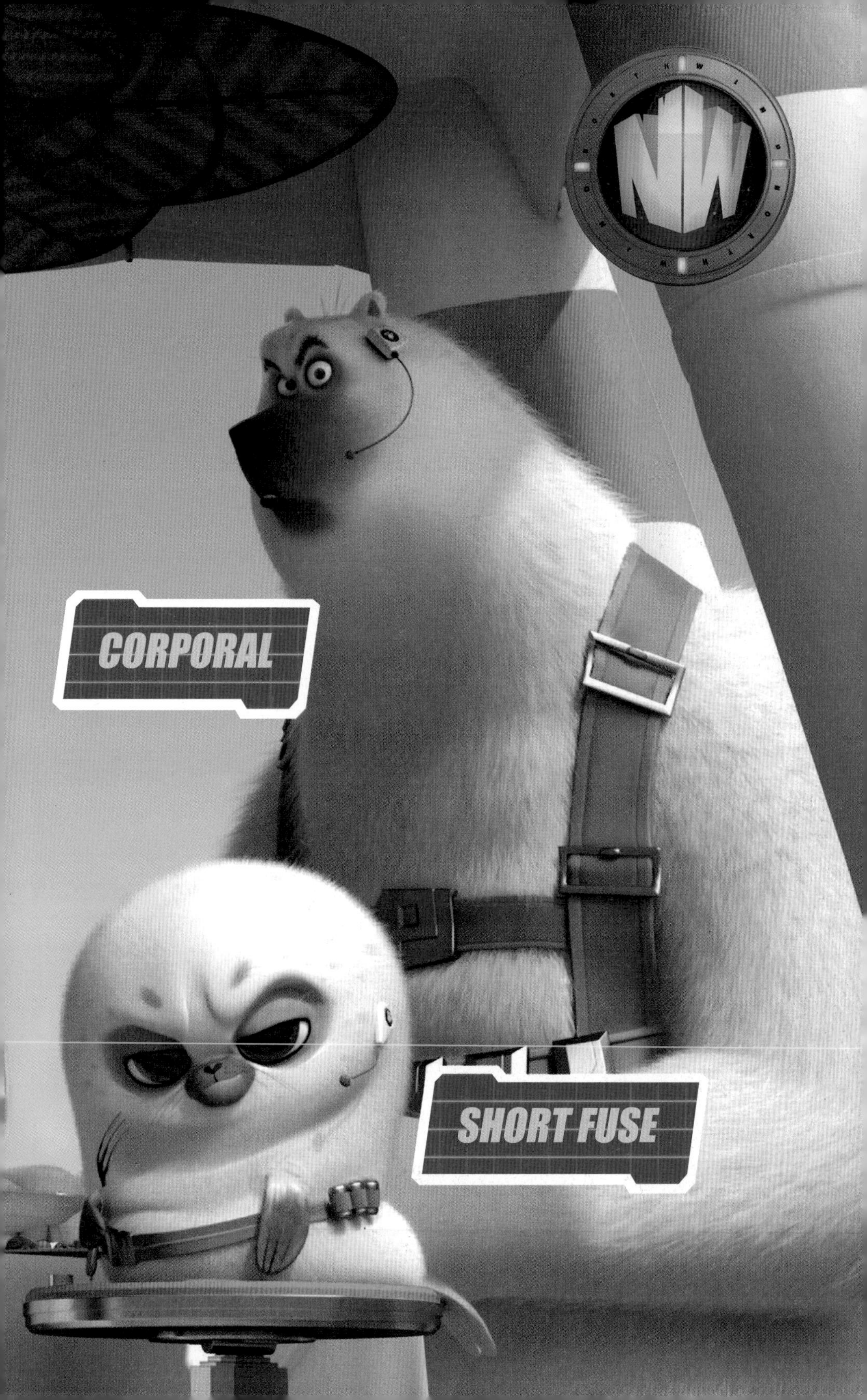

CORPORAL
SHORT FUSE

THE NORTH WIND in *Broken* PART ONE

WRITER **David Baillie** ARTIST **Grant Perkins**
LETTERS **Jim Campbell**

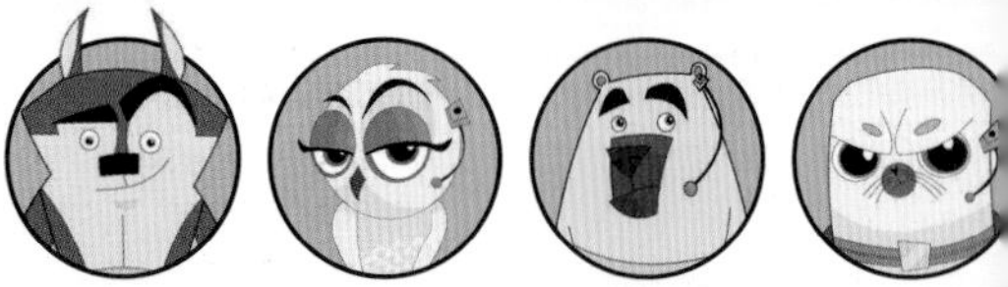
CLASSIFIED
EVA
CORPORAL
SHORT FUSE

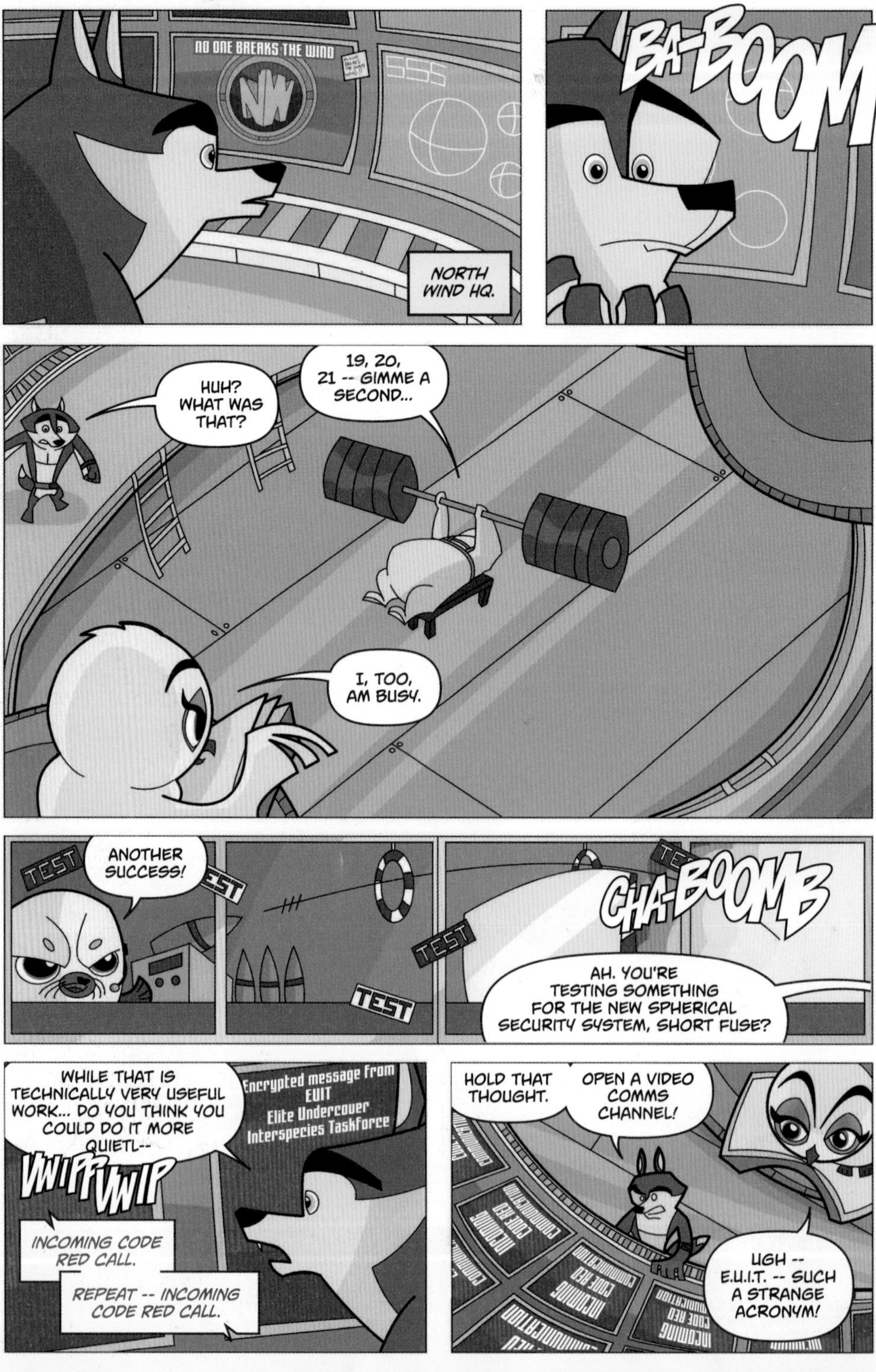
NO ONE BREAKS THE WIND
NORTH WIND HQ.
BA-BOOM
HUH? WHAT WAS THAT?
19, 20, 21 -- GIMME A SECOND...
I, TOO, AM BUSY.
ANOTHER SUCCESS!
TEST
TEST
TEST
TEST
TEST
CHA-BOOMB
AH. YOU'RE TESTING SOMETHING FOR THE NEW SPHERICAL SECURITY SYSTEM, SHORT FUSE?
WHILE THAT IS TECHNICALLY VERY USEFUL WORK... DO YOU THINK YOU COULD DO IT MORE QUIETL--
Encrypted message from EUIT Elite Undercover Interspecies Taskforce
VWIPPVWIP
INCOMING CODE RED CALL.
REPEAT -- INCOMING CODE RED CALL.
HOLD THAT THOUGHT.
OPEN A VIDEO COMMS CHANNEL!
UGH -- E.U.I.T. -- SUCH A STRANGE ACRONYM!

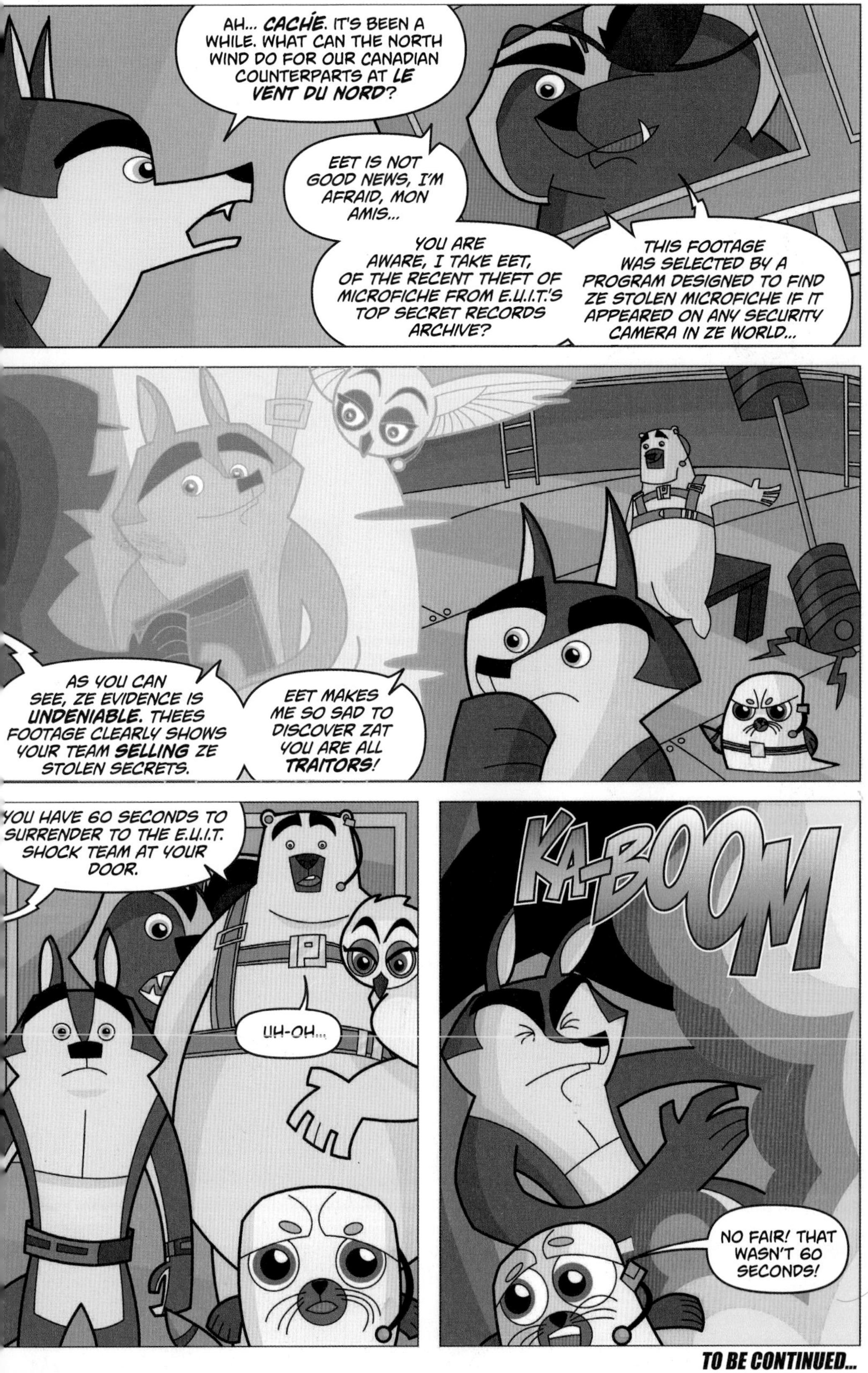

AH... CACHÉ. IT'S BEEN A WHILE. WHAT CAN THE NORTH WIND DO FOR OUR CANADIAN COUNTERPARTS AT LE VENT DU NORD?
EET IS NOT GOOD NEWS, I'M AFRAID, MON AMIS...
YOU ARE AWARE, I TAKE EET, OF THE RECENT THEFT OF MICROFICHE FROM E.U.I.T.'S TOP SECRET RECORDS ARCHIVE?
THIS FOOTAGE WAS SELECTED BY A PROGRAM DESIGNED TO FIND ZE STOLEN MICROFICHE IF IT APPEARED ON ANY SECURITY CAMERA IN ZE WORLD...
AS YOU CAN SEE, ZE EVIDENCE IS UNDENIABLE. THEES FOOTAGE CLEARLY SHOWS YOUR TEAM SELLING ZE STOLEN SECRETS.
EET MAKES ME SO SAD TO DISCOVER ZAT YOU ARE ALL TRAITORS!
YOU HAVE 60 SECONDS TO SURRENDER TO THE E.U.I.T. SHOCK TEAM AT YOUR DOOR.
UH-OH...
KA-BOOM
NO FAIR! THAT WASN'T 60 SECONDS!

TO BE CONTINUED...

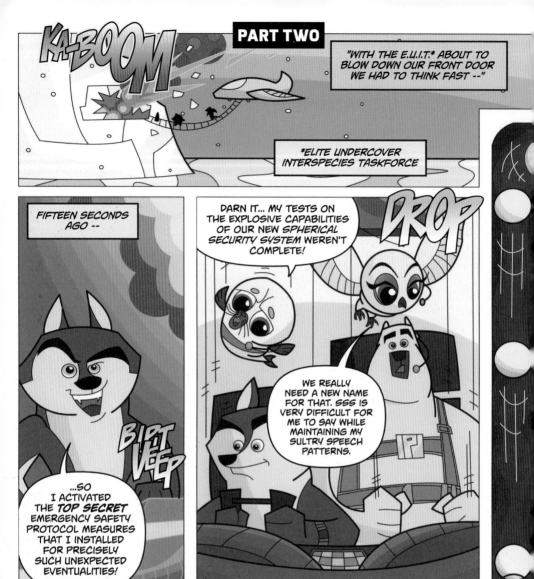

PART TWO

KA-BOOM!

"WITH THE E.U.I.T.* ABOUT TO BLOW DOWN OUR FRONT DOOR WE HAD TO THINK FAST --"

*ELITE UNDERCOVER INTERSPECIES TASKFORCE

FIFTEEN SECONDS AGO --

DARN IT... MY TESTS ON THE EXPLOSIVE CAPABILITIES OF OUR NEW SPHERICAL SECURITY SYSTEM WEREN'T COMPLETE!

DROP

BIP IT VEEP

...SO I ACTIVATED THE *TOP SECRET* EMERGENCY SAFETY PROTOCOL MEASURES THAT I INSTALLED FOR PRECISELY SUCH UNEXPECTED EVENTUALITIES!

WE REALLY NEED A NEW NAME FOR THAT. SSS IS VERY DIFFICULT FOR ME TO SAY WHILE MAINTAINING MY SULTRY SPEECH PATTERNS.

DID WE EVER COME UP WITH A *CODENAME* FOR THIS ONE?

YES. WE CALLED IT THE *SUBTERRANEAN LOCALISED INDESTRUCTIBLE NESTED GROUNDBREAKING SPECIALLY HYPER-DESIGNED OVOID TRANSPORTER.*

S.L.I.N.G.S.H... HANG ON -- WHY?

"NO REASON!"

CHUCK

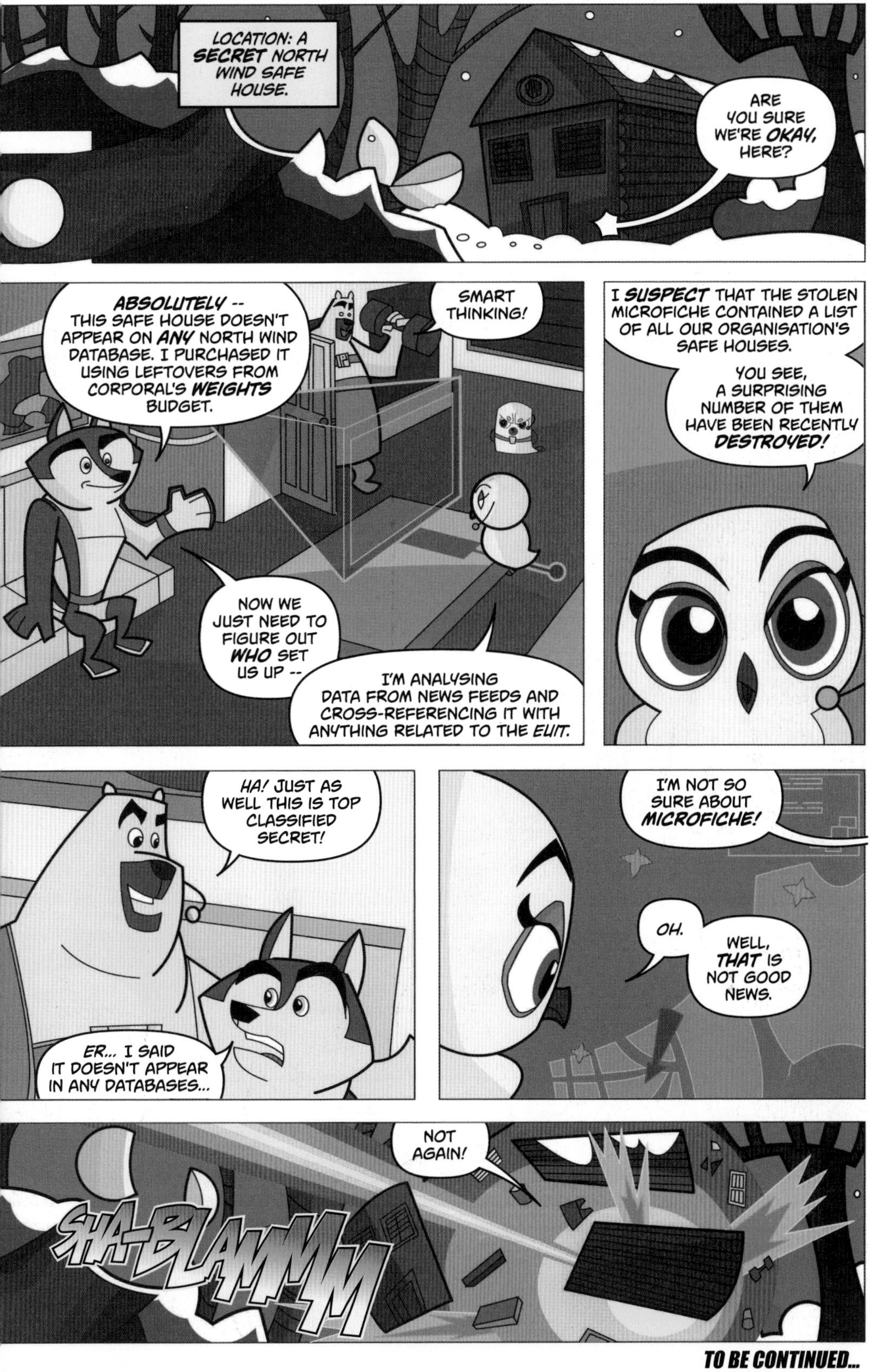
LOCATION: A SECRET NORTH WIND SAFE HOUSE.
ARE YOU SURE WE'RE OKAY, HERE?
ABSOLUTELY -- THIS SAFE HOUSE DOESN'T APPEAR ON ANY NORTH WIND DATABASE. I PURCHASED IT USING LEFTOVERS FROM CORPORAL'S WEIGHTS BUDGET.
SMART THINKING!
NOW WE JUST NEED TO FIGURE OUT WHO SET US UP --
I'M ANALYSING DATA FROM NEWS FEEDS AND CROSS-REFERENCING IT WITH ANYTHING RELATED TO THE ELIT.
I SUSPECT THAT THE STOLEN MICROFICHE CONTAINED A LIST OF ALL OUR ORGANISATION'S SAFE HOUSES.
YOU SEE, A SURPRISING NUMBER OF THEM HAVE BEEN RECENTLY DESTROYED!
HA! JUST AS WELL THIS IS TOP CLASSIFIED SECRET!
ER... I SAID IT DOESN'T APPEAR IN ANY DATABASES...
I'M NOT SO SURE ABOUT MICROFICHE!
OH.
WELL, THAT IS NOT GOOD NEWS.
NOT AGAIN!
SHA-BLAMMMM

TO BE CONTINUED...

PART THREE

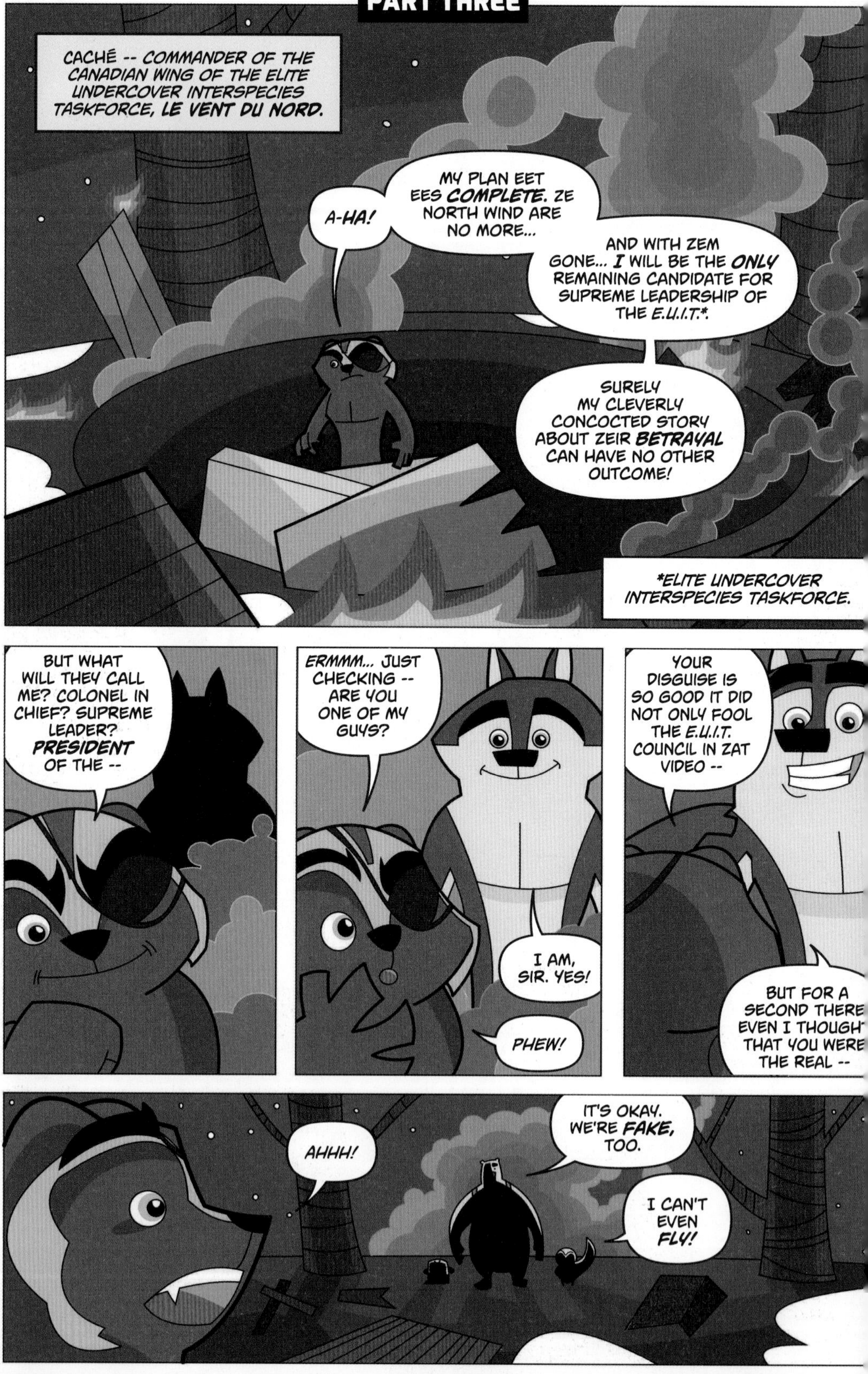

CACHÉ -- COMMANDER OF THE CANADIAN WING OF THE ELITE UNDERCOVER INTERSPECIES TASKFORCE, **LE VENT DU NORD.**
A-**HA!**
MY PLAN EET EES **COMPLETE.** ZE NORTH WIND ARE NO MORE...
AND WITH ZEM GONE... *I* WILL BE THE *ONLY* REMAINING CANDIDATE FOR SUPREME LEADERSHIP OF THE *E.U.I.T.**.
SURELY MY CLEVERLY CONCOCTED STORY ABOUT ZEIR **BETRAYAL** CAN HAVE NO OTHER OUTCOME!
*ELITE UNDERCOVER INTERSPECIES TASKFORCE.
BUT WHAT WILL THEY CALL ME? COLONEL IN CHIEF? SUPREME LEADER? **PRESIDENT** OF THE --
ERMMM... JUST CHECKING -- ARE YOU ONE OF MY GUYS?
I AM, SIR. YES!
PHEW!
YOUR DISGUISE IS SO GOOD IT DID NOT ONLY FOOL THE *E.U.I.T.* COUNCIL IN ZAT VIDEO --
BUT FOR A SECOND THERE EVEN I THOUGH THAT YOU WERE THE REAL --
AHHH!
IT'S OKAY. WE'RE **FAKE,** TOO.
I CAN'T EVEN **FLY!**

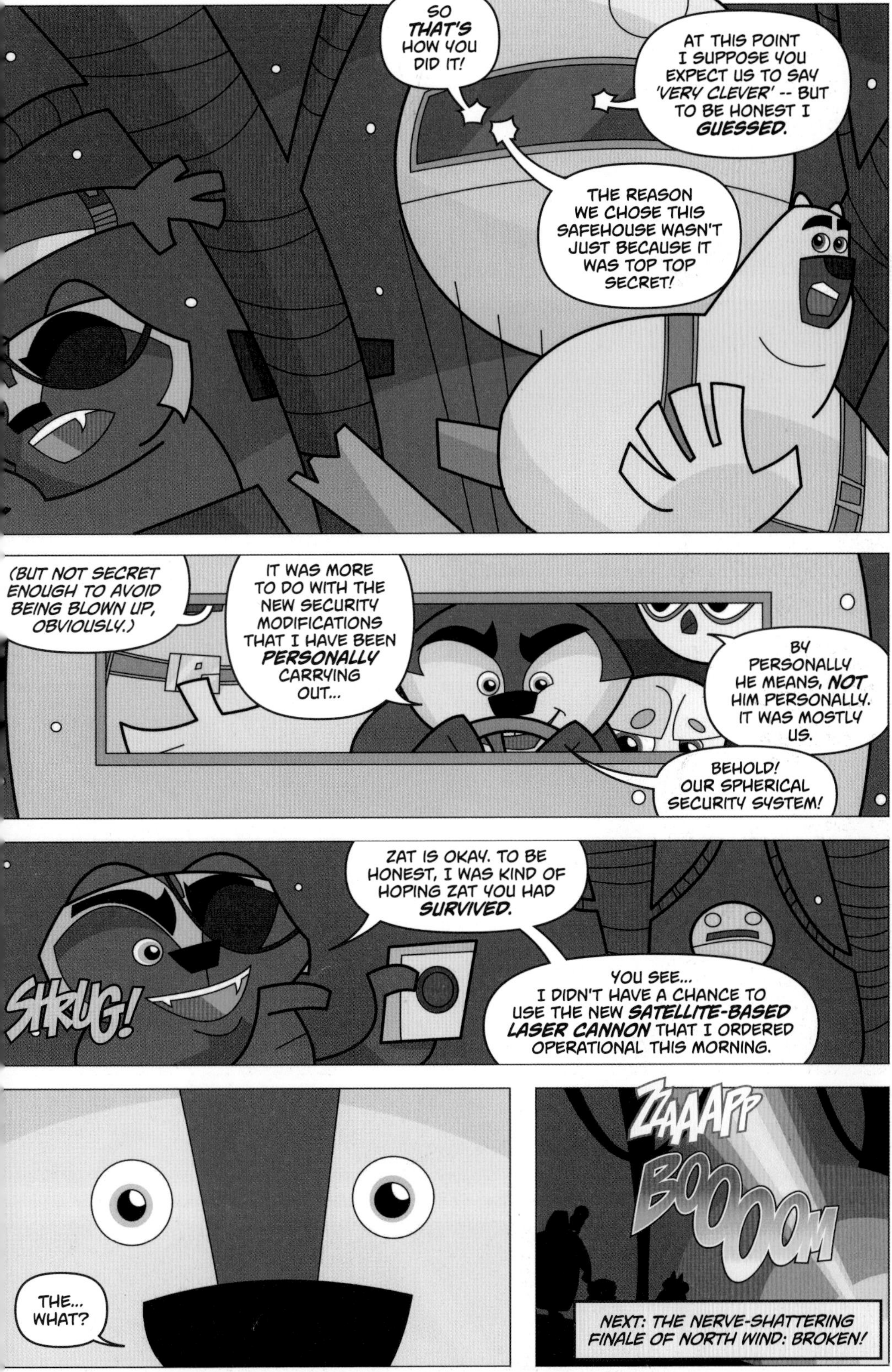
SO THAT'S HOW YOU DID IT!
AT THIS POINT I SUPPOSE YOU EXPECT US TO SAY 'VERY CLEVER' -- BUT TO BE HONEST I GUESSED.
THE REASON WE CHOSE THIS SAFEHOUSE WASN'T JUST BECAUSE IT WAS TOP TOP SECRET!
(BUT NOT SECRET ENOUGH TO AVOID BEING BLOWN UP, OBVIOUSLY.)
IT WAS MORE TO DO WITH THE NEW SECURITY MODIFICATIONS THAT I HAVE BEEN PERSONALLY CARRYING OUT...
BY PERSONALLY HE MEANS, NOT HIM PERSONALLY. IT WAS MOSTLY US.
BEHOLD! OUR SPHERICAL SECURITY SYSTEM!
SHRUG!
ZAT IS OKAY. TO BE HONEST, I WAS KIND OF HOPING ZAT YOU HAD SURVIVED.
YOU SEE... I DIDN'T HAVE A CHANCE TO USE THE NEW SATELLITE-BASED LASER CANNON THAT I ORDERED OPERATIONAL THIS MORNING.
THE... WHAT?
ZZAAAPP
BOOOOOM
NEXT: THE NERVE-SHATTERING FINALE OF NORTH WIND: BROKEN!

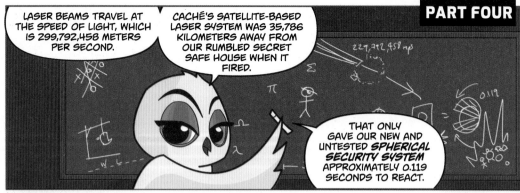

PART FOUR

LASER BEAMS TRAVEL AT THE SPEED OF LIGHT, WHICH IS 299,792,458 METERS PER SECOND.

CACHÉ'S SATELLITE-BASED LASER SYSTEM WAS 35,786 KILOMETERS AWAY FROM OUR RUMBLED SECRET SAFE HOUSE WHEN IT FIRED.

THAT ONLY GAVE OUR NEW AND UNTESTED *SPHERICAL SECURITY SYSTEM* APPROXIMATELY 0.119 SECONDS TO REACT.

SNAP

WELL, THAT WAS CLOSE.

"WHICH WAS PLENTY OF TIME. YOU KNOW -- CONSIDERING I CODED ITS REACTION CIRCUITS."

JUST IN CASE ANYONE FAILED TO NOTICE... I SAVED US.

YOU CAN ALL THANK ME LATER.

I THINK WE NEED A BIT MORE ROOM TO OPERATE!

PRESS

AND THEN, WITH THE PUSH OF A BUTTON...

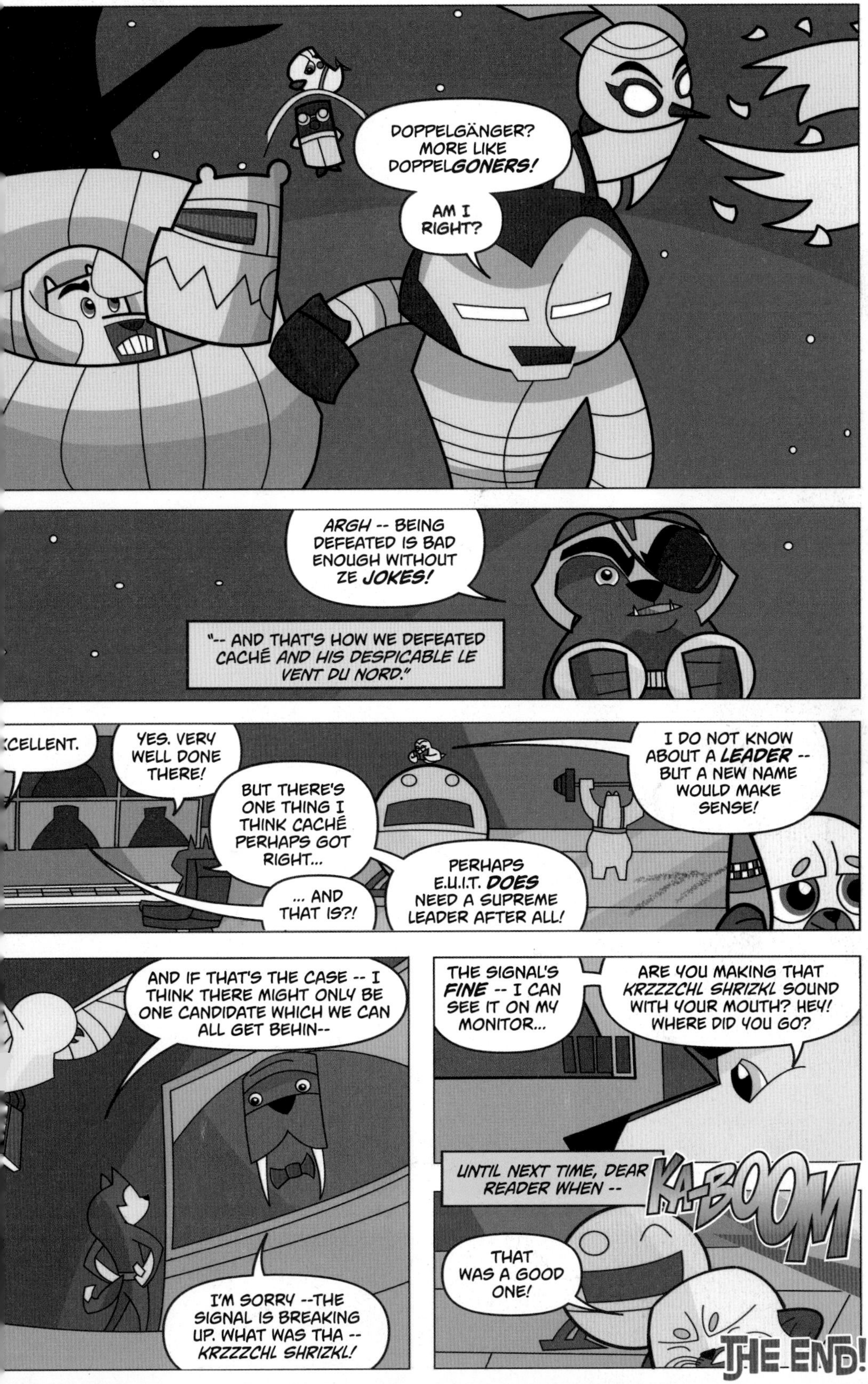
DOPPELGÄNGER? MORE LIKE DOPPELGONERS!
AM I RIGHT?
ARGH -- BEING DEFEATED IS BAD ENOUGH WITHOUT ZE JOKES!
"-- AND THAT'S HOW WE DEFEATED CACHÉ AND HIS DESPICABLE LE VENT DU NORD."
CELLENT.
YES. VERY WELL DONE THERE!
BUT THERE'S ONE THING I THINK CACHÉ PERHAPS GOT RIGHT...
... AND THAT IS?!
PERHAPS E.U.I.T. DOES NEED A SUPREME LEADER AFTER ALL!
I DO NOT KNOW ABOUT A LEADER -- BUT A NEW NAME WOULD MAKE SENSE!
AND IF THAT'S THE CASE -- I THINK THERE MIGHT ONLY BE ONE CANDIDATE WHICH WE CAN ALL GET BEHIN--
I'M SORRY --THE SIGNAL IS BREAKING UP. WHAT WAS THA -- KRZZZCHL SHRIZKL!
THE SIGNAL'S FINE -- I CAN SEE IT ON MY MONITOR...
ARE YOU MAKING THAT KRZZZCHL SHRIZKL SOUND WITH YOUR MOUTH? HEY! WHERE DID YOU GO?
UNTIL NEXT TIME, DEAR READER WHEN --
KA-BOOM
THAT WAS A GOOD ONE!
THE END!

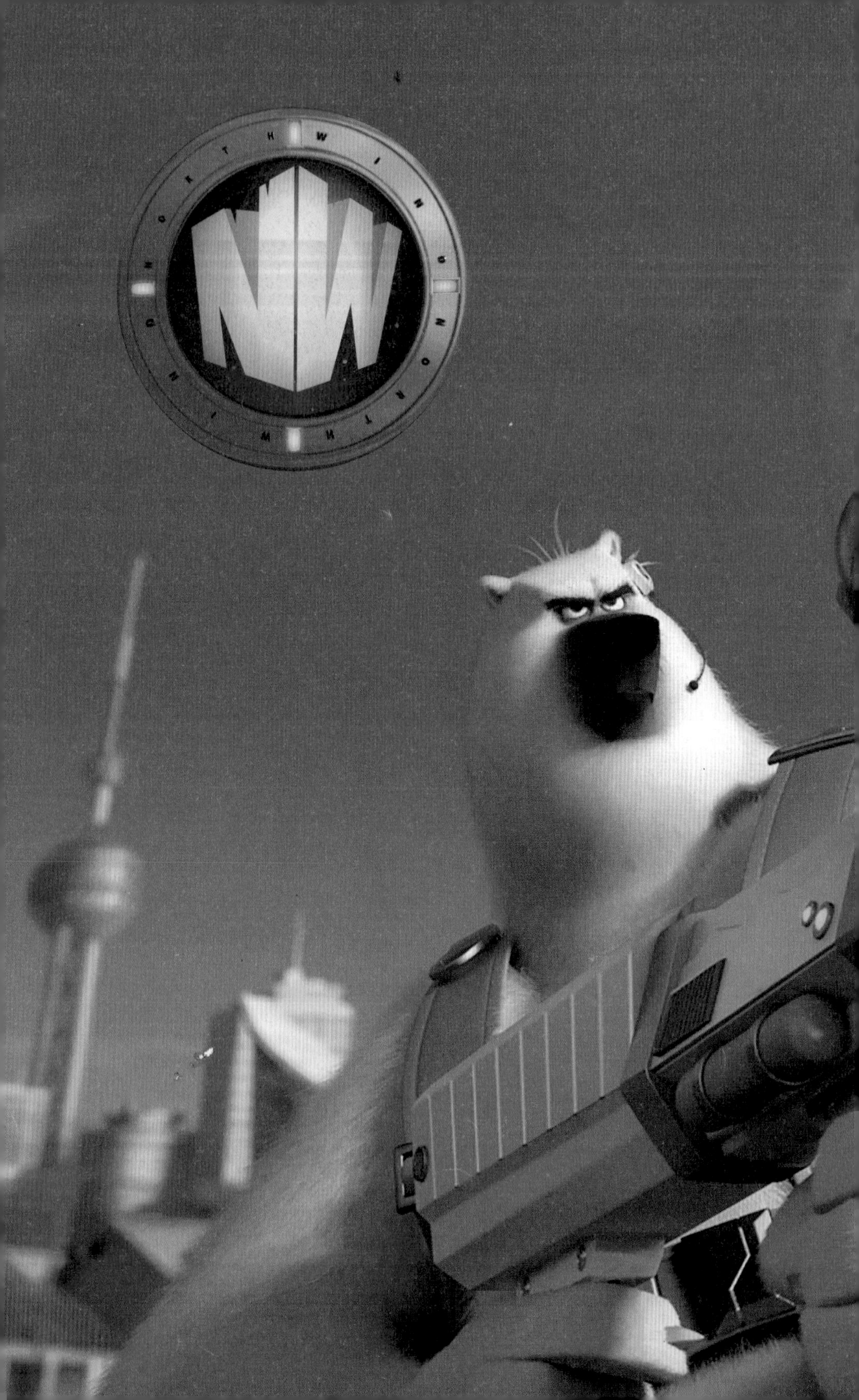

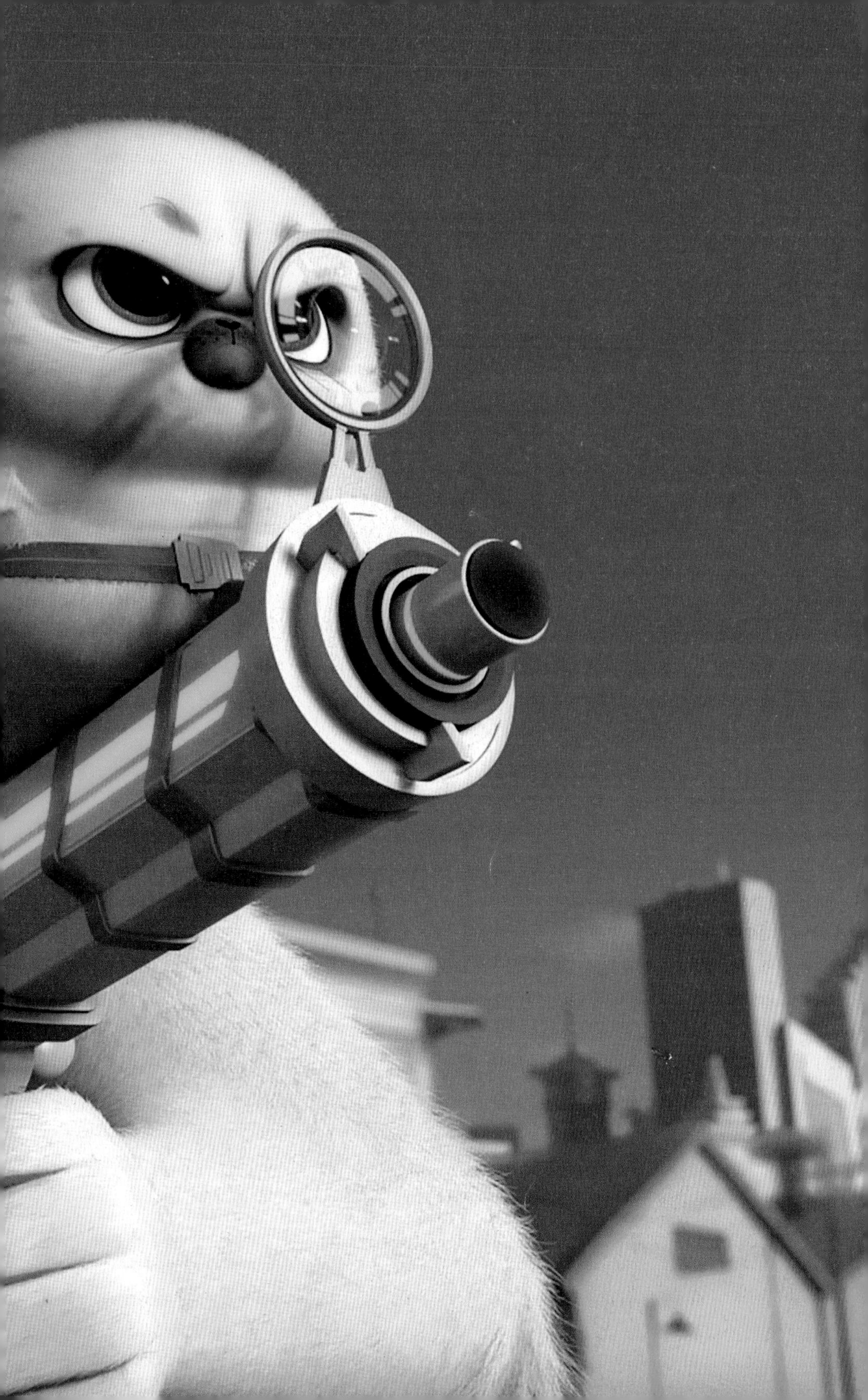

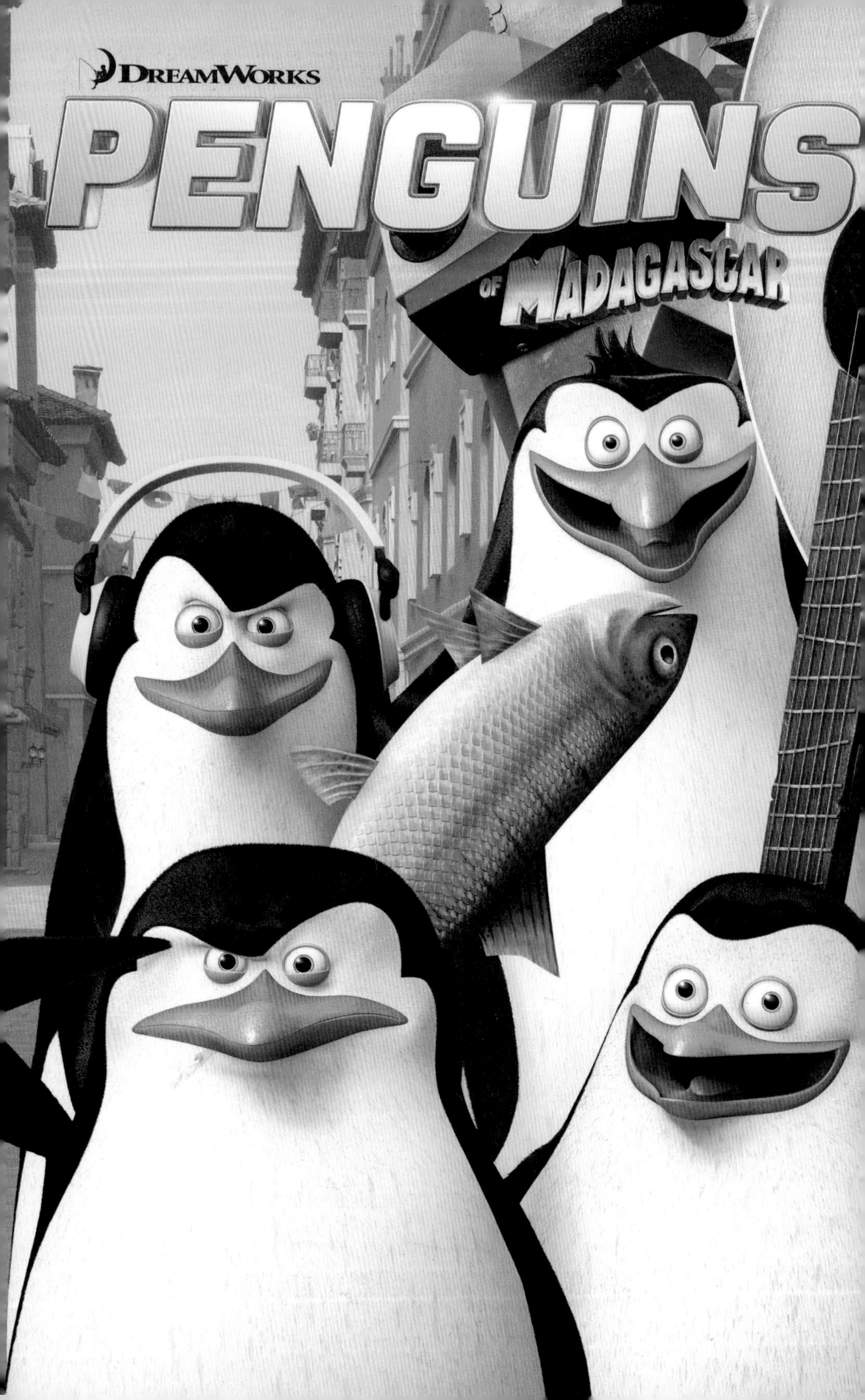
DreamWorks
PENGUINS
OF MADAGASCAR

TITAN COMICS GRAPHIC NOVELS

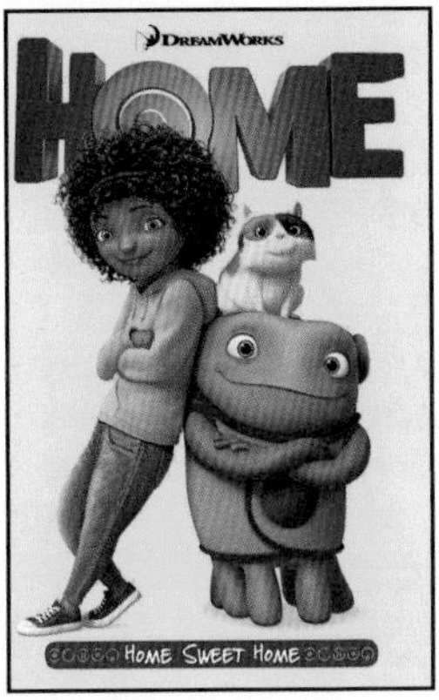
DreamWorks
HOME
Home Sweet Home

HOME: HOME SWEET HOME

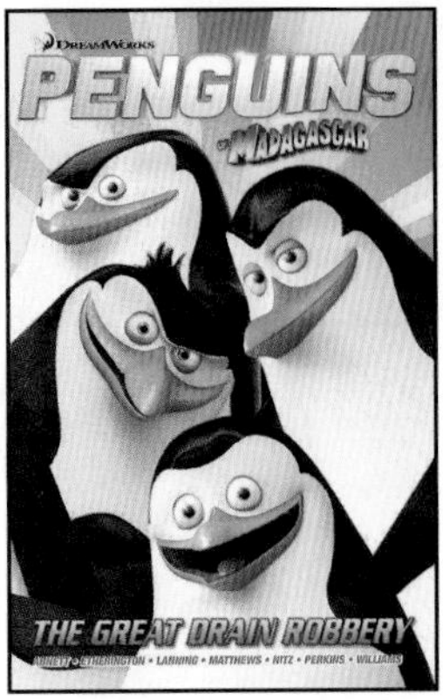
DreamWorks
PENGUINS
of MADAGASCAR
THE GREAT DRAIN ROBBERY

PENGUINS OF MADAGASCAR:
THE GREAT DRAIN ROBBERY

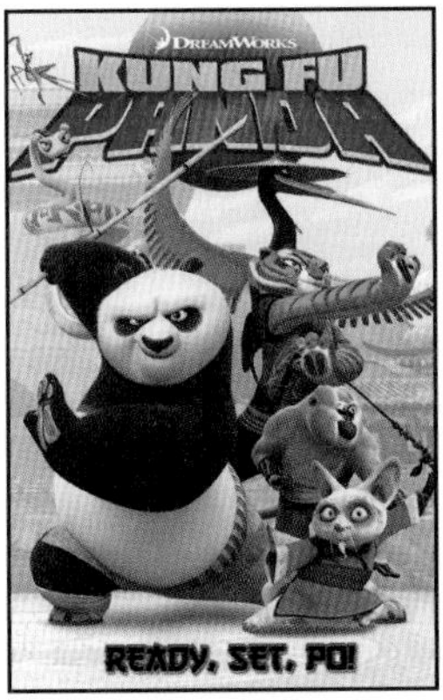
DreamWorks
KUNG FU PANDA
READY, SET, PO!

KUNG FU PANDA –
READY, SET, PO!

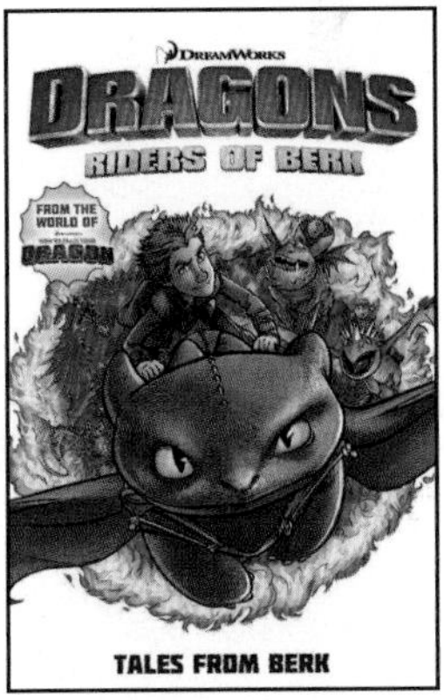
DreamWorks
DRAGONS
RIDERS OF BERK
FROM THE WORLD OF
TALES FROM BERK

DREAMWORKS DRAGONS:
RIDERS OF BERK – TALES FROM BERK

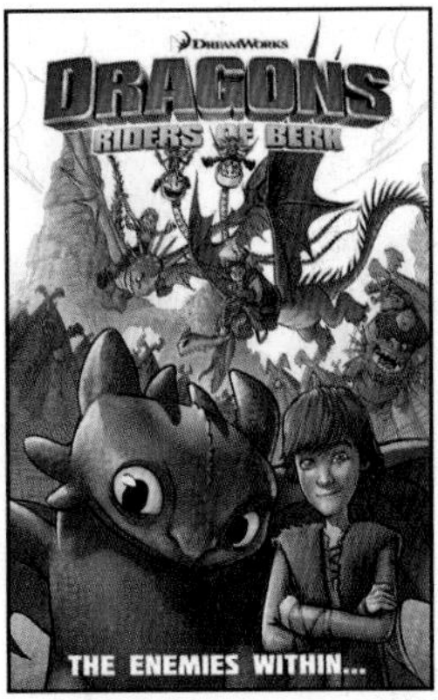
DreamWorks
DRAGONS
RIDERS OF BERK
THE ENEMIES WITHIN...

DREAMWORKS DRAGONS:
RIDERS OF BERK – THE ENEMIES WITHIN

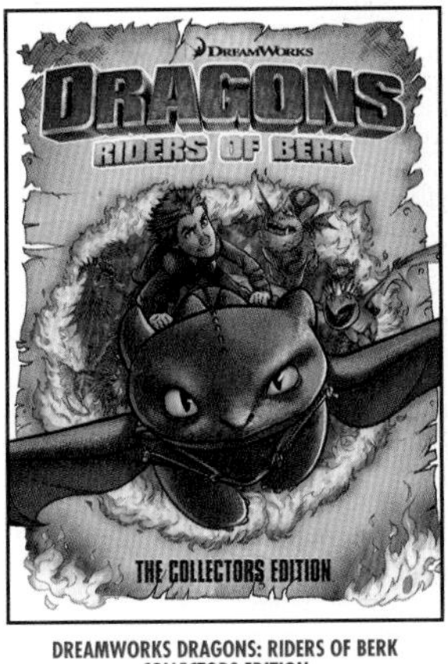
DreamWorks
DRAGONS
RIDERS OF BERK
THE COLLECTORS EDITION

DREAMWORKS DRAGONS: RIDERS OF BERK
COLLECTORS EDITION

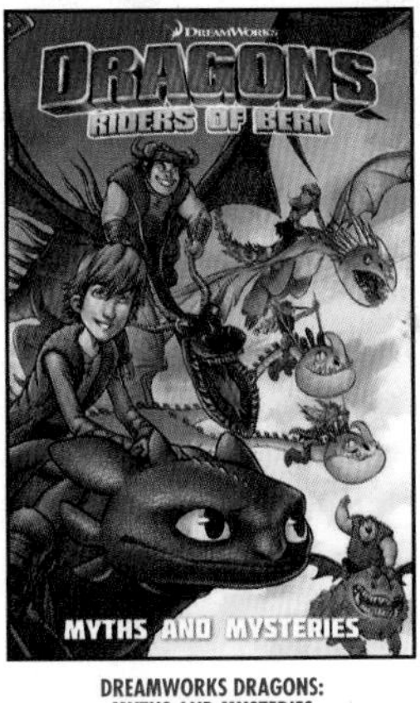
DreamWorks
DRAGONS
RIDERS OF BERK
MYTHS AND MYSTERIES

DREAMWORKS DRAGONS:
MYTHS AND MYSTERIES
COMING SOON

WWW.TITAN-COMICS.COM

TITAN COMICS

DreamWorks ANIMATION SKG

TITAN COMICS COMIC BOOKS

AVAILABLE MONTHLY NOW!
ALSO AVAILABLE DIGITALLY.
WWW.TITAN-COMICS.COM

The Adventures of Puss in Boots © 2016 DreamWorks Animation LLC. All Rights Reserved.

TITAN COMICS DIGESTS

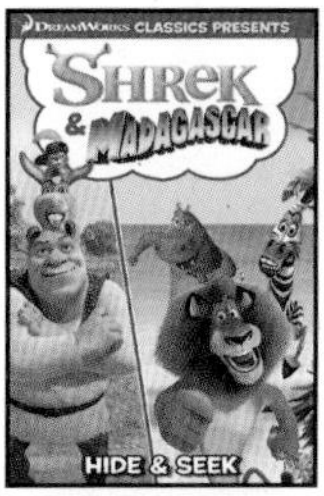
DreamWorks CLASSICS PRESENTS
SHREK
& MADAGASCAR
HIDE & SEEK

Dreamworks Classics – 'Hide & Seek'

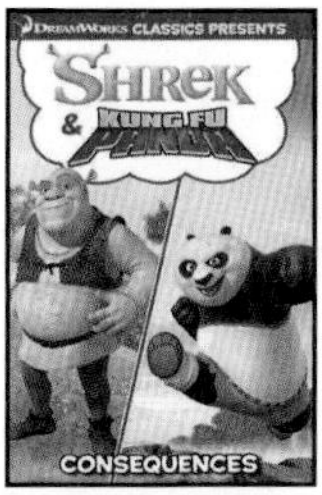
DreamWorks CLASSICS PRESENTS
SHREK
& KUNG FU PANDA
CONSEQUENCES

Dreamworks Classics – 'Consequences'

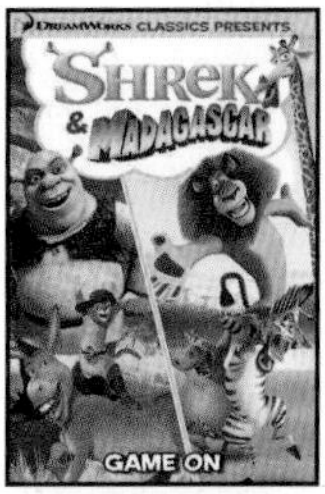
DreamWorks CLASSICS PRESENTS
SHREK
& MADAGASCAR
GAME ON

Dreamworks Classics – 'Game On'

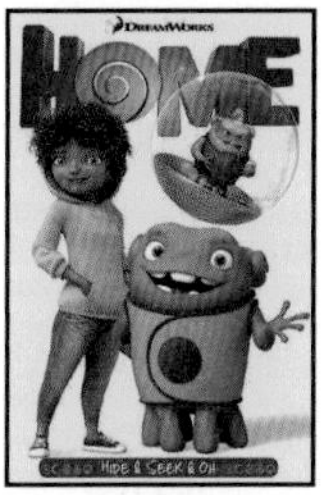
DreamWorks
HOME
HIDE & SEEK & OH

Home – Hide & Seek & Oh

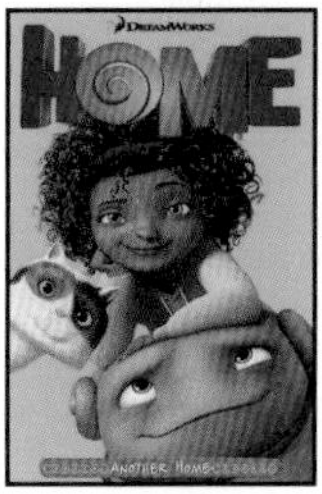
DreamWorks
HOME
ANOTHER HOME

Home – Another Home

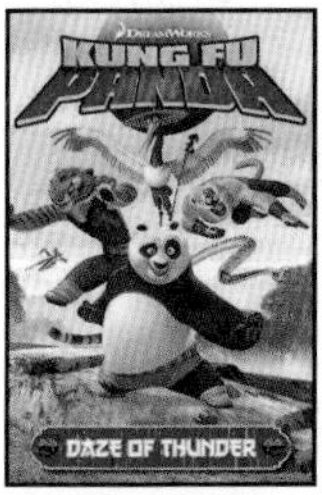
DreamWorks
KUNG FU PANDA
DAZE OF THUNDER

Kung Fu Panda – Daze of Thunder

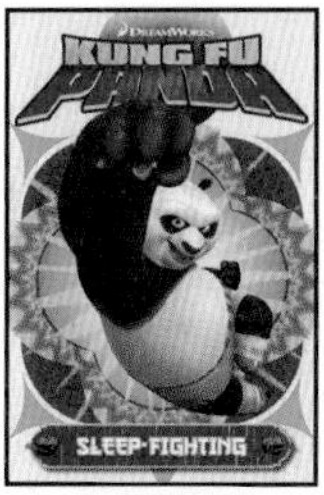
DreamWorks
KUNG FU PANDA
SLEEP-FIGHTING

Kung Fu Panda – Sleep-Fighting

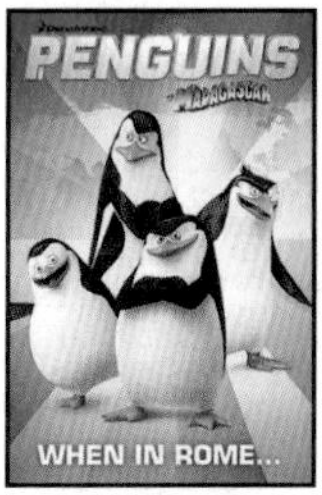
PENGUINS
OF MADAGASCAR
WHEN IN ROME...

Penguins of Madagascar – When in Rome...

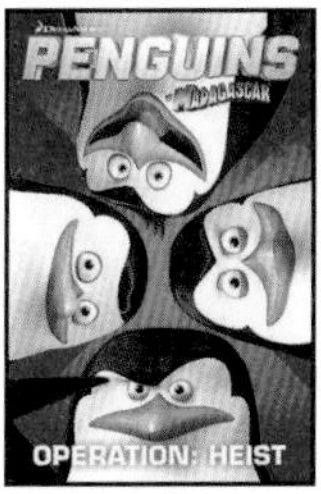
PENGUINS
OF MADAGASCAR
OPERATION: HEIST

Penguins of Madagascar – Operation: Heist

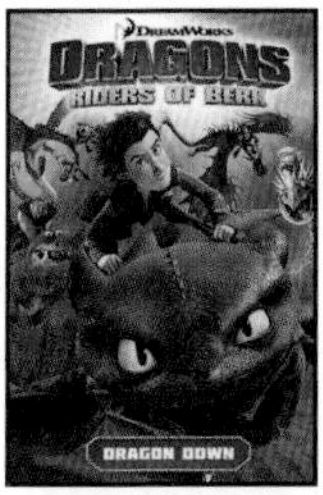
DreamWorks
DRAGONS
RIDERS OF BERK
DRAGON DOWN

DreamWorks Dragons: Riders of Berk – Dragon Down

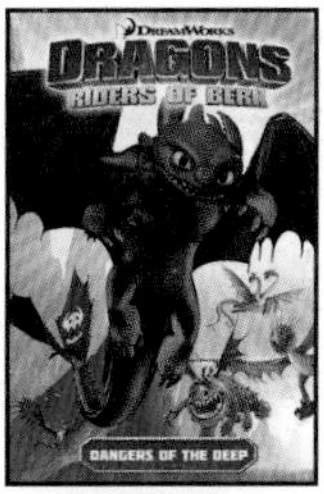
DreamWorks
DRAGONS
RIDERS OF BERK
DANGERS OF THE DEEP

DreamWorks Dragons: Riders of Berk – Dangers of the Deep

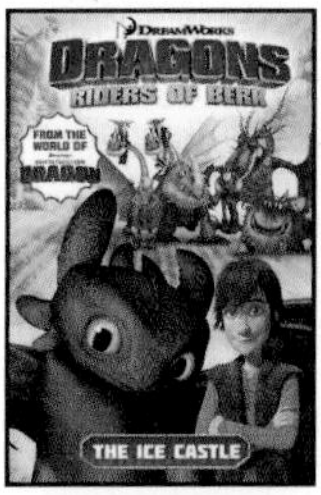
DreamWorks
DRAGONS
RIDERS OF BERK
THE ICE CASTLE

DreamWorks Dragons: Riders of Berk – The Ice Castle

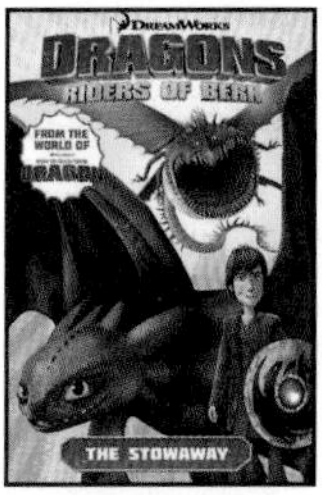
DreamWorks
DRAGONS
RIDERS OF BERK
THE STOWAWAY

DreamWorks Dragons: Riders of Berk – The Stowaway

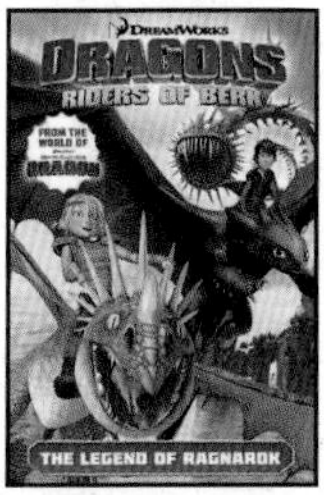
DreamWorks
DRAGONS
RIDERS OF BERK
THE LEGEND OF RAGNAROK

DreamWorks Dragons: Riders of Berk – The Legend of Ragnarok

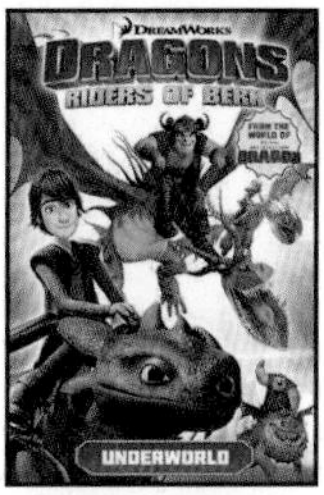
DreamWorks
DRAGONS
RIDERS OF BERK
UNDERWORLD

DreamWorks Dragons: Riders of Berk – Underworld

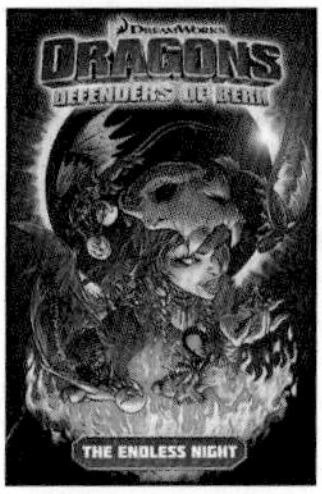
DRAGONS
DEFENDERS OF BERK
THE ENDLESS NIGHT

DreamWorks Dragons: Defenders of Berk - The Endless Night

WWW.TITAN-COMICS.COM

ALSO AVAILABLE DIGITALLY